ACT NORMAL

Also by Greg Hollingshead:
Bedlam
The Healer
The Roaring Girl
Spin Dry
White Buick
Famous Players

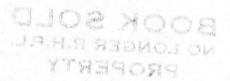

ACT NORMAL

STORIES

GREG HOLLINGSHEAD

Published in Canada in 2015 by House of Anansi Press Inc.

House of Anansi Press
110 Spadina Avenue, Suite 801
Toronto, ON, M5V 2K4
Tel. 416-363-4343
Fax 416-363-1017
www.houseofanansi.com

House of Anansi Press is committed to protecting our natural environment.
As part of our efforts, the interior of this book is printed on paper that contains
100% post-consumer recycled fibres, is acid-free, and is processed chlorine-free.

19 18 17 16 15   1 2 3 4 5

"Wing Night" has appeared in different form (as "The Assistant") in *Prairie Fire*
and "The Drug Friendly House" in *Eighteen Bridges*.

Library and Archives Canada Cataloguing in Publication

Hollingshead, Greg, author
Act normal : stories / Greg Hollingshead.

Issued in print and electronic formats.
ISBN 978-1-77089-970-4 (pbk.).—ISBN 978-1-77089-971-1 (html)

I. Title.

PS8565.O624A65 2015   C813'.54   C2015-902069-7
                                           C2015-902070-0

Book design: Alysia Shewchuk
Typesetting: Marijke Friesen

 Canada Council   Conseil des Arts
for the Arts   du Canada

 ONTARIO ARTS COUNCIL
CONSEIL DES ARTS DE L'ONTARIO
an Ontario government agency
un organisme du gouvernement de l'Ontario

*We acknowledge for their financial support of our publishing program
the Canada Council for the Arts, the Ontario Arts Council, and the Government of Canada through the Canada Book Fund.*

Printed and bound in Canada

MIX
Paper from
responsible sources
FSC   FSC® C004071
www.fsc.org

For David and Rosa

Gleeson: Is this another denial?
Gravano: It's not a denial. It's just a way of talking.
    — *The Gotti Tapes*

Q. How "wasted" is really wasted, and do you foresee it?
A. No, I don't foresee it, but it's more or less like a ruthless
   type of feeling. Very ruthless and intoxicated to a degree.
    — Bob Dylan interview

CONTENTS

UNBOUNDED

When Al was in the picture, Dorry Cronshaw's energy mostly went into the relationship. When Al left her for a twenty-three-year-old named Tiffany, Dorry's horizons expanded to include all the things that were wrong with her life. One of these was her backyard fence, which Al might have got around to replacing if he hadn't replaced her first. She googled *fencers*, thinking something in Cape Cod Grey, six feet in back, three in front.

I'll need a paint chip, the guy from Lorne's Wood Fence said when he called back right away. Nobody's touched Cape Cod Grey for years. Benjamin Moore's Pilgrim Haze or Pike's Peak's the closest you'll come. You can take it from there. Just remember it's not exactly the acme of fashion right now. And it'll look bluer once it's up.

He took her address.

When the quote arrived, it was too high the way a figure will exceed your wildest expectation by only so much.

Dorry got two more quotes. The first arrived with apparent reluctance and was nearly twice the one from Lorne's Wood Fence. The other came scrawled in pencil on the back of an envelope stuffed under her back door in the night. The Lorne's Wood Fence quote was starting to look pretty good, but she couldn't afford it. And then she remembered she had neighbours on both sides.

Carlotti, to the north, had recently stripped the decking from his front porch. She caught him balanced on the exposed joists removing his front door. He set his power screwdriver on the doorsill and stood looking down at her. She pointed to the decking piled on his front walk and said,

Mike, see all those exposed nails? What about the mailman? What about the kids at Halloween?

Halloween is a wild time, Carlotti said.

Dorry outlined her hopes for a new fence.

Here's what, Carlotti said. I take down the old one, you put up your new one.

Am I made of money? Dorry said. What's your arrangement on the other side?

I don't remember.

So Pinchbeck paid. A good fence on both sides, and you put in nothing?

Okay, fine. Carlotti reached for his screwdriver. Get quotes and check back with me.

I already got quotes.

Just for the back, right? Nobody fences their front yard. A hedge, maybe. Bougainvillea makes a nice hedge.

Standing on the front step of the Kazoleases' bungalow on Dorry's south side was like standing before a vent in a savoury pie. For someone feeling like a homemaking failure, it was an olfactory slap in the face.

When Mrs. Kazoleas failed to invite her in, leaving Dorry to speak into the darkness on the other side of the screen door, Dorry said, I warn you, Mrs. Kazoleas, this conversation will be strained.

Silence, which deepened as Dorry disparaged the state of their mutual fence. Perhaps Mrs. Kazoleas had gone to check on a pie. But as soon as cost-sharing came up, she was right there, declaring what a good fence it was.

Come with me, Dorry said. I want to show you.

But Mrs. Kazoleas had commitments indoors. She would speak to Mr. Kazoleas.

What the hell. Dorry left a message with Lorne's Wood Fence.

‹ ‹ ‹

Ten days later, at 7 a.m. on the dot, a lean man in faded jeans and a T-shirt stood at Dorry's back door looking unhappy.

Good fences make good neighbours, Dorry said.

It's more complicated than that.

She held out her hand. You must be Lorne.

Yeah, I do my own work.

As they sat at her kitchen table and "went over the quote," Dorry wondered if he was prickly and morose because he feared things would not go well but when the job was done and she had expressed her satisfaction and he had folded her cheque into his wallet and was packing up, his cheerful side would show through. Or if it was something else. Something older and bigger. Ingrained.

What if you run into problems? she asked.

What kind of problems?

Oh, I don't know. Tree roots? A body? *Hah!*

Lorne looked at his watch. He was missing the tips of two fingers on his left hand.

Lorne's Wood Fence, Dorry said. I like that. Frank. To the point. No fooling around.

He shrugged. It's a lazy name.

When can you start?

I'm here. I've started.

‹ ‹ ‹

By the end of Wednesday, Dorry's old fence was piled alongside the garage. The next day she took a flex day, and while Lorne dug postholes down the windowless side of the house, she baked a carrot cake and iced it warm. The icing went translucent on top, ran down the sides of the cake, and hardened in a moat around the base. She backed out her door with this and tea things on a tray. When she swung round, the glare and sensory blast of the day nearly forced her back inside.

Later she decided it was not an unwanted mid-morning break to be served incompetently iced carrot cake on a patio in full view of the neighbours while the client yammered like a ditz that had Lorne remote and ill at ease. He was remote and ill at ease for other reasons.

Finally, he placed his hands on his knees, elbows spread, a man about to rise, and said,

So you still want three feet?

What?

In front.

Two feet?

You don't need anything in front.

My neighbour Carlotti thinks a bougainvillea.

Nobody fences their front lawn. Not around here.

I'd hoped to.

I don't advise it.

But you're a fencer.

Meaning I fence appropriately. I know what's right for a neighbourhood. I know what people do, what won't antagonize the people around them, what they won't regret. A fence is an important decision.

That day he dug a few more holes and left at dusk with the posts in and his old truck stacked with Dorry's rotten fencing. Watching him pull away, she thought, Now, there goes a man of integrity. Difficult, absolutely, but on principle. And then she thought, I irritate him.

The next day at the office she imagined her fence going up while she got on with things here, and life felt efficient, productive, full almost, or like what full almost used to feel like. But that night when she got home there was no sign Lorne had even been there.

He's juggling two jobs, she reflected. Look how fast he called back, and then he couldn't start for ten days. He came here while waiting on supplies for some other job, and now they've arrived and he's had to go back to that one. He's self-employed, saying yes to every opportunity, because when you're freelance it's feast or famine. Did I ever say the job was urgent? He'll show tomorrow — except tomorrow's Saturday. But all these guys work weekends now.

Home from work Monday and still nothing, she left a message on Lorne's machine.

On Tuesday, Mrs. Kazoleas came to Dorry's back door smelling like a spice bazaar. Mr. Kazoleas had agreed to pay for half the fence on their side.

That's great, Dorry said. Terrific. Thanks. When Mrs. Kazoleas remained standing there looking grim, Dorry said, What? What is it?

A problem. With the fence down meanwhile, Dorry's clothesline was visible from the window over the Kazoleases' kitchen sink, and twice that week Mr. Kazoleas had come away from the dishes enflamed.

Kitchen floor is hard, Mrs. Kazoleas said. Please, dry underwear inside.

As Dorry agreed to Mrs. Kazoleas's request, she understood that Mr. Kazoleas had been given no choice in the matter of payment for half the fence on their side.

Lorne called Friday.

Where have you *been*? Dorry asked him.

I'm waiting for my friend the psychologist to come over.

Why? What's wrong?

I'm a little down.

I thought you were on another job.

I'm not up to one job, at this point.

Half days? Take it easy?

I'm taking it easy. If I didn't have a phone on my bed table, we wouldn't be having this conversation. My cell's dead. I don't even know where it is. I'll see what my friend says and come when I can.

Meanwhile, Dorry had a row of posts but no fence. Across the back lane she now had a long view of the Nordstroms' backyard. Neat but sparse, a little military. No shrubbery, grass trimmed to within an inch of its life. Brown patches. A nothing-coloured shed, a concrete pad with a corrugated yellow fibreglass roof on rusted poles, for the Dodge Caravan. Vlad's telescope set up on the patio, pointing at the sky, never used.

To Dorry's left, the Kazoleases' backyard was a carpet of ground plants with tendrils now extending into her yard. To her right, instead of the former aluminum siding and shingled roof of Carlotti's garage, she saw raw boards under a ripped blue plastic tarp billowing and flapping in the wind. With the fence down, she could see discarded shingles in a mound next to the trench Carlotti had dug on three sides of a two-car garage now resembling a dust bowl shack. She could also see the firewood he'd turned his beautiful weeping birch into, as well as a pile of used bricks next to a heap of jagged concrete. From inside the house came prolonged blasts of a jackhammer. Occasionally Carlotti would stagger out coated in dust, with a chunk of concrete in a canvas apron. He seemed to be breaking up his basement floor, possibly in order to pave it with the flagstones he had stacked by his back door, a renovation she had never heard of anybody undertaking.

The next day, as they worked in their respective gardens with no fence between them, Dorry and Mrs. Kazoleas fell into conversation. When Dorry asked what she did with all her vegetables, Mrs. Kazoleas told her that some she canned and the rest she and Mr. Kazoleas sold on weekends at the farmers' market, where they specialized in relishes and pies. When the conversation came round to the fence, Dorry assured Mrs. Kazoleas that she'd soon have one again, but when Mrs. Kazoleas said nothing, her hands continuing to move expertly, ruthlessly, among her plants, Dorry wondered if she wasn't kidding herself, or lying.

So your husband, Mrs. Kazoleas said. He is away on long trip?

That night Lorne called to ask if Dorry would be up for a little Jeremy Taylor.

I sure would. Where's he playing?

Author of *Holy Living*, 1650.

Jeepers creepers! Hold on while I turn off the iron.

Look upon pleasures, not as they come toward you to be enjoyed, Lorne read in a sepulchral voice, *for then they paint and smile and dress themselves up in tinsel and glass: but when thou hast rifled and discomposed them with enjoying their false beauties, then behold them in their nakedness and weariness. See what a filthy carcass they discover and be no more abused.*

When Dorry didn't say anything to this, Lorne asked her what she was thinking.

She was thinking how long it had been since anybody had rifled and discomposed her false beauties. It's not exactly life-affirming, is it? was how she expressed this. If your *before*'s false, chances are pretty good your *after*'ll be disgusting. And isn't every life form a filthy carcass? Doesn't everybody shit and die? Is this the guy who thought his craps smelt like violets?

No, you're thinking of Henry More, the Platonist.

The next night, Dorry was standing on a chair changing a bulb over her bathroom mirror when she happened to glance down, and without a fence she could see straight into Carlotti's TV room, and there he was, naked as a newborn but hairier, squirming on a reclined La-Z-Boy. What was he doing? She got the binoculars. He was using pliers to remove the piping around the footrest.

The following day, Carlotti called from his backyard to borrow Dorry's hammer. At first she thought *jack*hammer and looked at him. I broke my spare one, Carlotti explained. He held up an ordinary hammer with a broken claw.

I didn't know hammers did that, Dorry admitted as she handed him hers. Aren't you just taking out nails?

Carlotti's hands were shaking from all the jackhammering, and he was pancaked with dust. Some do, he said.

Mike, why are you dismantling everything you own?

He didn't seem to understand the question. She rephrased it.

I'm fixing up, he said, finally.

Preparing to. You're breaking all your eggs at once. But you *are* making an omelette, right?

I enjoy working on my property.

The next day, Lorne emailed her a poem he'd written himself. Entitled "Joy Ride to Black," it opened with a comparison between the escalating expansion of the universe and the escalating pace of modern life and closed with the darkness of the sky after the earth has outdistanced the light from the nearest star as an image of the darkness in the hearts of men.

Wait a minute, Dorry thought. The nearest star's the sun. We'll still have daylight. A little muted, but still. Not wishing to encourage Lorne and yet reluctant to lie, she waited two days before calling. She got his machine.

Three days later he called back, saying, I just picked up your message.

You're a poet, she said, and kicked herself.

You probably thought that was the depression talking, but it wasn't, it was me taking the long view. You know what a ha-ha is?

No.

A ditch for a fence, to open up the space to the eye. First used in English deer parks. Big on eighteenth-century estates. On the property side you'd have a masonry retaining wall. You've seen them.

I don't think so.

Why use good wood for a fence when you can dig one? Also, somebody needs to invent a retractable home roof. A house convertible. People in bed should be able to look up at the sky.

Talk to Carlotti. He'll have yours off in a week.

Air jets to keep out dust and insects. Birds and bats. Light rain. Dew. Also, public lighting should be outlawed after midnight. Light pollution's wreaking havoc on people's sleep patterns, among other things.

My neighbour Vlad'll drink to that. He's an amateur astronomer and alcoholic.

Lorne didn't say anything.

Reeking? Is that how you pronounce it? Lorne, come when you can. But I do have no fence.

You don't need a fence. Not in the larger scheme of things.

I'm exposed here. We all are. We need our fence.

You want the truth? Put up a fence and you create a barrier. Inside a barrier anything can happen. With no fence you've got the security of the public gaze. We think we can go on building fences, but we can't. The world isn't divided up, it's in pieces, and who broke it? A fence is ketchup on a tomato. A trashed tomato.

Lorne, all I know is I shouldn't have to get dressed to go out into my own backyard.

With a fence you go out naked?

Of course not. I wear my dressing gown.

That's different. Jack Benny went back onstage wearing a dressing gown after every show, and he had millions of people watching. This was sixty years ago.

Lorne, it's your responsibility to replace the fence I had until you took it away, which you did on the understanding that you would build me another one. We practically signed a contract on this.

‹ ‹ ‹

Two days later, a truck from Tim-Br Mart dropped off a load of eight-foot one-by-six pressure-treated boards. The next day Lorne was back. Using a stain that matched perfectly the paint chip Dorry had found that matched perfectly her vivid recollection of Cape Cod Grey from Augusts camping on the Cape with Al the first few years after they were married, Lorne stained the boards on a sawhorse he set up on a canvas tarp at the bottom of the yard and nailed them up as they dried. There were not enough in the load to fence the front. By late afternoon two Mondays later, he was finishing the back gate. It was now late October, three days to Halloween. As Lorne worked into the dusk on Friday, Mrs. Kazoleas came to Dorry's front door carrying a giant pumpkin.

For you, she said. Draw mouth, eyes, use Magic Marker, or paint, don't cut, then you make nice dish. Soup, pie, anything. Men will enjoy.

Tearing, Dorry swore that she would.

At the end of the next day, the job done, Lorne knocked at Dorry's back door.

The fence looks great, she said.

It's a little blue.

He'd warned her, but she'd assumed he thought she was stupid. The kid at the paint store had warned her too, but she thought, Just like a man, and what is he, seventeen?

Lorne was holding a rough-hewn jewellery box in dark wood that had many compartments, each with a little brass handle. Extending it to her, he said,

For your tinsel and glass.

Why, Lorne — Tearing again.

At Dorry's kitchen table, as she opened and closed the drawers of the box, Lorne told her how, seven weeks before this, the night before he got her first message, he'd had a 3 a.m. call from his old high school friend Horse, on a cellphone from a mountaintop in Nepal. It was a call from the past, from deep space. Solar winds. Horse was driving his girlfriend Carly down the mountain to see a doctor about a pain in her stomach. Suddenly Carly straightened in her seat and turned as if to say something, as if she'd just had a terrific idea. Instead, she laid her temple on the dashboard and went into convulsions. Horse pulled off the road and held her as she died.

Oh my God, Lorne, those poor people — What was it?

Lorne shook his head.

Will Horse be coming back to Canada? Dorry asked next, after a silence.

No. That was one of the things they had talked about over the next few weeks. Lorne held up his left hand, the one missing the tips of two fingers. When I first started in the business, he said, I wasn't sure fencing was for me, and then I lost these to it.

You hate fences.

It's more like I'm ambivalent.

Lorne's Ha-Ha?

Nobody would understand.

Lorne's Ditch?

Come on.

How long were Horse and Carly in Nepal?

Five years next month. Horse has an export business. And now that he's lost Carly to the place . . . When Horse called, Lorne continued, he told me they'd sent me something. A few days later I got a parcel notice from the post office saying the postman rang but there was no answer. There was no answer because the postman didn't ring. I was home. I heard him come up the steps, I heard him put the parcel notice and my other mail in the box, and I heard him go down the steps. He didn't ring.

I know, Dorry said. You're lucky these days if the postman rings once.

So I go down to the post office, Lorne said. When they see my name on the notice, they call the postmaster, who takes me into the back. There's nobody around. We sit at the staff lunch table, and he tells me about Canada Post and its *contract with the customer.* As he's talking he's turning the parcel in his hands. I can see Nepalese stamps and that it's been opened and resealed. He finishes by saying Canada Post isn't Canada Customs, but he's looking forward to the day when the two corporations are working hand in glove. Then he slides the parcel across the table at me. I drove home looking over my shoulder.

Your postmaster thinks Canada Customs is a corporation?

Lorne indicated the box. So what it was was this and a letter from Carly.

Did Carly know how ill she was?

They both knew she had something. Horse thought it was a mountain thing.

She said that?

No, he did, when he called.

Can I ask you what Carly's letter said?

She was happy. She had pain and she was losing weight, but she was happy. Mostly she wrote about going up the valley with the locals for the hash harvest. Kneeling to rub the stalk of the plant until the pollen sticks to the palms of your hands. The locals were better at it, ten times faster, but her technique was improving every day. Even just half an ounce takes forever. You scrape it off your palms and roll it into sticky little balls.

She left you for him?

Listen. Horse and Carly looked out for each other just fine.

Of course they did, Dorry thought. *What do I know?* Lorne, she said, thank you so much for this beautiful gift.

Lorne rubbed hard at his face. When he took his hands away, there were red spots on his cheeks, like circles of rouge. He looked beat. There was no dope, he said. Somebody at the post office took it for himself. Or they shared it. No new truck for me for a while.

Anyway, Dorry said.

Listen. Do you want to go get something to eat?

Lorne, I'd love that. I'd whip us up something here, but all I've got's this — And Dorry turned in her chair to indicate the pumpkin Mrs. Kazoleas had given her. It was sitting on the kitchen counter beside them, too orange, too weightless-looking. It was mammoth. It could have been a stage prop, in papier mâché, shellacked fifteen times.

From the way Lorne was looking at it, he had never seen anything like it.

It needs a face, Dorry said, but a drawn one, not cut, and she told him that as soon as Halloween was over she planned to try out some pumpkin dishes, with advice from Mrs. Kazoleas. I've been collecting recipes, she said. Today I even picked up the Autumn Baking issue of *Gourd Housekeeping*.

Lorne didn't laugh. He said *Huh* and looked at her with his eyebrows lifted. Then he looked back at the pumpkin.

I'll paint my face, Dorry said. And we can go.

I'll be here, Lorne said. He was still looking at the pumpkin.

THE RETREAT

This year they were trying something different: separate vacations.

Ten days up there doing that is insane, his wife said as they were packing.

Not as insane as ten days at a spa in the Mojave Desert in August.

Eight days. Sonoran Desert. How many times do I have to tell you?

The retreat was held in an abandoned high school on the edge of a small town in northern Ontario. The men arrived from all over the province, as well as from Manitoba, Quebec, and the northeastern US. Most were middle-aged. Quite a few looked younger than their Birkenstocks. Everybody's waking time was mostly spent in the full lotus on yoga mats in the gym. Those, like him, incapable of the full lotus, sat along the walls on the moulded fibreglass seats of school desks with the table part sawn off. He kept catching his sweats on the ragged stump. The day started at four-thirty in the morning and ended at ten-thirty at night. It consisted of three four-hour meditation sessions; two hours of Buddhist instruction from a CD; three macrobiotic meals served in the former cafeteria; a bedtime snack of granola with organic soy set out on teachers' desks ranged down the central hallway; and six hours' sleep on mats in empty classrooms, twenty mats to a classroom. All this in silence, except for the instruction, the shuffling, the snuffling, the coughs, the belly rumbles, the farts, the snores. Communication by erasable black marker on a whiteboard on the gym wall. After three days everybody was shitting pure compost.

Participants were required to agree in writing to stay the full ten days. No visitors allowed. No trips out. Upon arrival, participants reported to what had once been the principal's office. There they surrendered all keys, phones, and any other electronic devices. On the first evening, he submitted a whiteboard request for the temporary return of his car keys. He'd left his pillow on the passenger seat. The organizers, serious long-haired men with the air of super-annuated camp counsellors, didn't like it, but they handed over the keys.

In the parking lot, he discovered that all the cars had been parked in a tight block ten vehicles square. Why was not clear. It was a big lot, there was no shortage of space. Also unclear was why, considering that he had not been among the first to arrive, his car was one of the four at the centre of the square. The cars were so tightly parked that somebody appeared to have set himself a Zen task. It was necessary to take off his shoes and socks and climb onto the hood of the outer car nearest his and across four roofs to the roof of his. From there, when he tried to reach down to unlock the passenger door, he nearly slid off onto his head. So he descended to the hood and so to the ground and squeezed far enough past the passenger door to unlock it and, with difficulty, nearly pulling a muscle, reach his pillow. After retracing his route, he returned the keys. No eye contact, disapproving silence. Later, on his mat that first night, waiting for sleep, he watched the arrival of the first of many thoughts concerning this perverse and inexplicable arrangement with the cars.

‹ ‹ ‹

In the meditation sessions, the idea was non-judgemental awareness. You watched your breathing. When you noticed you had thinking going on, in the same way that you'd been watching your breathing, you paid attention to the thinking and any emotion it brought with it, and then you let it all go. (*Die to it* is how the voice on the CD put it, a formulation that made him a little uncomfortable.) The next thing you knew you had thinking going on again. Again you paid attention and let it go. The next thing you knew, *etc.* It was shocking how easily and often, even here, doing this, he kept finding himself once again lost in thought, heading down old familiar thought-gullies. *Wadis*, the cassette called them. Arroyos. Periodic floodways.

By Night Five, as he stretched out on his mat for the fifteen seconds before sleep came rushing in, he was spending probably three or four seconds two or three hundred times an hour paying attention. It wasn't much, but even so, his powers of awareness had become so acute that he was tracing the vocal nuances of a nearby wolf pack as it ranged nightly through the schoolyard and down the valley. He could feel in his lungs the carcinogens from the bleach used to disinfect the place, and he could sense, like brain tickles with form, familiar contours of old thought and replayed emotion, a sad fear-fraught, pleasure-seeking mindscape. He'd known it all before, of course, but forever caught in the flow down this or that ditch, he had lost sight of what it felt like to climb out once in a while. Here, doing this, he knew again. He'd pay attention — climb out — and the next thing he knew he was back *wadi*-sunk, as before.

For a novice, two or three days of this sort of thing would have been a better idea. Stick a toe in. Five days would have been pushing it. By mid-morning of Day Seven, that parking arrangement had become a *wadi* the size of the Elora Gorge. For some time he'd been picking up faint jinglings from the sweats pockets of certain meditators, and while palpably oversensitized, he was pretty sure he knew what he was hearing: car keys, quietly returned to a select few. Soon everybody would have their keys back. Even, eventually, him. And yet, owing to the uncanny placement of his car in the block of vehicles, almost everybody would be able to leave before him. This meant that even when his own keys were physically in his hand, thirty-six of these men would be able to leave but not him. When the thirty-six had left, another twenty-eight would be able to drive away but not him. After the sixty-four had departed, twenty would be free to go but not him. In fact, the number of participants who could leave before he could was even greater than the number of parked cars would suggest. Some had carpooled. A party of twelve had arrived by chartered bus. According to the whiteboard, it would be picking them up. One guy, outfitted like an African explorer, had arrived by helicopter. He could leave from the roof if he wanted, like Special Forces.

On his way to dinner the evening of Day Eight, he left a note on the whiteboard demanding the *immediate extrication* of his car from the *nightmare autogrid*. It was the kind of notice board message that leaves nobody in any doubt that someone in the group has cracked and can blow at any time. When he returned from dinner, which each time he came to attention he found himself shovelling down in a rage, somebody had erased his demand and in its place written the following:

Note that no participant car can be moved until 8 a.m. August 25.

Now, 8 a.m. August 25 would be the morning after the last official day of the retreat, viz., two days, fourteen hours, and fifteen minutes from now. And that was just when the whole departure process was scheduled to *begin*. He must have been expecting a more accommodating response.

The next part — him taking out his disappointment on the whiteboard and the wall — he doesn't fully remember.

He paused and turned. Silence. The shouting, kicking, and hammering had ended. His tormentors faced him in a half-circle. Scraps of whiteboard lay scattered across the floor between him and them. One of his tormentors was speaking in a calming voice while making the gestures of a man suppressing a large balloon, and he thought, They'll be used to meditators who crack. It's not like they're novices. Novices would not have had the balls to charge 127 men this kind of money to travel at their own expense to sit for twelve hours a day for ten days in a derelict, hell-and-gone, un-air-conditioned, bleach-doused, wolf-ridden, probably condemned building, on a diet of rice, beans, cut-up Granny Smiths, granola, and soy milk, with their keys confiscated and their cars trapped in a nightmare autogrid.

The only question was how many of these goons he could kick to death before they beat him insensible.

He let this thought go.

Hyperventilated but otherwise calm, he followed a kid who worked in the kitchen to the office to find his keys and then out to the parking lot. If this was the Zen trainee who had parked the cars, he was now doing a remarkably effective impression of a laid-back doper. The kid moved four cars, and then his. When the kid slipped out of the driver's seat, he probably wasn't supposed to hand over the keys, but he did.

Calmly, he looked at them. Calmly, he climbed in and fishtailed out of there in the spirit of the angry teenage son of an abusive lumber baron father in the days when this was a high school. Twenty minutes down the highway, calmer now but driving too fast to stop in time, he did a squealing U-turn and drove back to a bar, a strip club by the look of it, set deep in a field of scrub. The Hot Pot, Spot, Shot, Slot. The Hot Something. A flashing beacon of rose-coloured neon. He pulled in. The parking lot was tufted like a mattress.

Inside, at a table near the stage, still wearing his meditation sweats, grateful for the low light, though nobody seemed to notice or care, he ordered the Philly Cheese Melt with Extra Large Fries and a bottle of Johnnie Walker Red. Leaned back in his seat and waited for the first show, due to begin in a little over an hour's time.

It seemed to him that veering off in this way was different from letting go of your thoughts, because instead you were consciously setting out to create a memory, which one day you would marvel at or be appalled by. Yet this way too was a shot at something actual, for a little while. Not kosher maybe, but real, and even true. And not only did it make a grateful change, but it helped to explain such otherwise unaccountable phenomena as his presence in this highway strip joint on this late August evening in his thirty-seventh year, just as it helped to explain the millions of shabby dives and steepled houses of worship scattered across the face of the earth. Because the question was not how many naked women a man needs to see before he dies, any more than it was how many naked Christs. The question was how can anybody spend their waking life sunk in *wadis* and not just as soon be asleep, or dead?

The first two did not do. If these were happy women, they were not happy about people seeing them without their clothes on. Even if it was only him in his torn sweats and a table of hipsters, or college kids with beards anyway, here ironically (but not disrespectfully), and a few solo bachelor cottagers and a lesbian couple, all sitting quietly in the dark. Not this evening. Maybe later tonight. Maybe ten years ago. This evening they behaved like women who had found it necessary to drape a towel over the dressing-room mirror before they climbed into their G-string.

He looked at his watch. If he had any sense he would drive back to the city right now. If he left immediately he could be home by dark. He could have the house to himself, for two days, or was it three? And do what? Watch his thoughts come up and let them go?

An hour later, the Johnnie Walker at the halfway mark, feeling significantly better, he was about to leave, feeling for his keys, when the third act, Miss Star Alliance, came on. Slowly he sat back down.

After her third and last set, which started at half past midnight and ended sometime after one, he invited Miss Star Alliance to his table. It was clear to him that behind the beautiful eyes set wide in that beautiful head atop those broad, shining shoulders, eyes that flashed and gleamed, that never stopped scanning the darkness, was a genuine, real-time person. They fell easily into conversation. When Miss Alliance spoke, she had a charming way of opening her mouth wider than she needed to, as if to fit her perfect whiter-than-white teeth around the unaccustomed words she was speaking to this unusual, sweats-garbed gentleman, who was also opening his mouth wide, perhaps in order to communicate with maximum winning precision how unutterably charming he was finding her.

‹ ‹ ‹

Later, when he woke on his stomach on a nicotine bedspread, he knew from the lump of his wallet under his thigh that Star Alliance was not a thieving whore. But where was he? The answer came from the bathroom mirror, printed on his cheek, in relief: *The Drop Inn*. He had slept on the plastic-relief oblong attached to his room key. Parting rayon curtains, he saw, across the highway, his car, didn't see it, saw it, didn't see it, under the flashing neon sign, the only vehicle in the Hot *Trot* lot. It was 4:05, still dark. The days were getting shorter.

He watched his thoughts come up. He let them go.

Sitting on the edge of the bed, emptying his pockets, he found the $610 bar receipt, with a phone number on the back in a schoolgirl hand. At noon, unable to sleep another minute, expecting a wrong number, a boyfriend, a pimp, a toddler, an adolescent, his finger shaking, he tried the number. When she answered on the first ring, he fell to his knees on the grimy carpet. Yes, of course she remembered him. No, she wasn't working today. Today was her day off. Her days off were so boring. Lunch? She would love to have lunch with him.

In a Greek restaurant in North Bay, he found Star Alliance to be, as he had sensed drunk, a real person, actual name Edith Lazaire, born of a seamstress mother, now deceased, father unknown, in Port-au-Prince, Haiti, thirty-four years ago. She could have said twenty-four, or forty-four, it was all the same to him. But Edith Lazaire knew better, and even he understood that even if she really was only thirty-four, then her dream of rue Ste-Catherine was nothing more. It was a cruel injustice that *Exotic Dancer* was the only box she could have ticked with hope of a Canadian visa. She had come to this country with — and had suffered since — real blows, real wounds, real losses, real injustices, real gaps in the record. None of it accountable by her. Not at the present time. Not a fraction of it. Questions made her gloomy. The more he pressed, the gloomier she became, until something shifted, and it was a different, more practical-minded woman who leaned toward him and said,

So what do you want?

Want? he said, surprised, and thought, Take you to lunch on your day off? Get to know the person behind the goddess on that stage last night? My holiday attempt to introduce some truth into my life so far proving fruitless, I thought I'd come at it another way?

You want in my pussy? she said. Because it seems like you want in my head. The head is not in the cards.

Beyond this, she needed him to know that she had no regrets. She would do it all again. Every last mistake she would make again, because it had been hers to make and no one else's, and that's how it would remain. And there was something else she needed him to know: he had already taken up an awful lot of her time, and she liked nice clothes. And shoes. Nice shoes.

He found this a depressing turn for the conversation to take, but it did explain the businesslike tone. He'd been telling himself that *A* was not what was going on here, it was strictly *B*, when in reality, from the very beginning, it had been *A* and nothing but *A*. Because it didn't matter what he did in his head with this, she and the world knew exactly what was going on here. In fact, most people over the age of eighteen born at any time since the Upper Paleolithic who saw the two of them eating lunch here at Tony's Acropolis would know what was going on here — though some, familiar with incarceration, or institutions more generally, would take note of the sweats and conclude psychiatric patient on a day pass with his nurse.

So he took her shopping. Put everything on his card, would need to pay and lose the statement before his wife saw it. What was he *doing*? This afternoon he was sitting on benches in various concourses of a North Bay mall outside dress shops and shoe stores watching the shoppers with their walkers and sport shoes and weight problems, watching his thoughts come up and letting them go, until he was once again hailed inside to pay. At some point in Hour Three, there was a problem with his card.

Sir, the woman at Visa said, your spending pattern's been showing up a little irregular here. Are you really at the Bayview Mall in North Bay?

Soon after putting Visa's fears to rest, he got Edith out of there. Took her for dinner at her favourite restaurant, a marble-and-red-velvet coliseum called La Scala Steak House, where nobody sang. It was a quiet meal. He took her home, a fire-escape walk-up over a Stedmans. When he said he probably should be getting along, she put her arms around his neck and whispered,

You know what I never told you I like to do? My favourite thing? Swallow.

No, I don't think you did tell me that. I'm sure I'd remember if you did. But actually, I need to get going.

Not surprisingly, Edith found this an extraordinary response to her intimate disclosure. She dropped her arms and took a step back, to see his face. Are you fucking with me?

He shrugged. I'm married.

You think I don't know that? You think I don't know you've had a hard-on for me for the last twenty-four hours? What is the *matter* with you?

I don't know. Maybe I love my wife.

Maybe, *maybe?* Shit.

Look, I'm sorry if I've —

The blow connected with the side of his head with enough force to convince him that she was the one hit. But before he could reach out to shield her from being hit again, it happened again, from the other side, an equally power-ful blow, and this time he thought *having ears boxed* and imagined a violent act of containment down an alley or per-haps canyon of pain, closer to the ground, and he thought *put in my place*, he was on his hands and knees though not for long, because with something of the strength he'd witnessed onstage, he was hauled back to his feet and given a shove and was outside, on the landing, and she was in the doorway, at the same time sweeter and more menacing than people generally are, saying, like a little girl, a crazy, tena-cious one, So you'll call me?

He said he would, but that these were ridiculous things for them both to be saying he knew from the way, as he stumbled down the stairs, she called after him, thanking him for the clothes and shoes spilling out of boxes scattered around the shabby room behind her.

‹ ‹ ‹

It was past midnight when he pulled into his driveway, but the lights were on. His wife was in the kitchen, with a tan, in a white blouse that set it off, a dark skirt, drinking coffee with somebody he had never seen before.

You're back, she said. You look terrible. What happened to your face?

You too. Back, I mean.

This is Sam, she said. Sam took me to a movie. Or I took Sam. Sam and I took each other to a movie.

Even as Sam, who also had a tan, equally deep, half turned in his chair, half rising, to shake his hand, a study in illness at ease, he said, Well, I guess this is my cue. When Sam stood up, he was taller than him and ten years younger. And then he left.

See you Monday, Sam, his wife said. She was getting up to put the mugs in the dishwasher. Thanks for the movie!

What was it? he said.

What was it called, Sam? she called, but the front door had already closed.

Who's Sam? he said.

A guy I work with.

You've never mentioned a Sam.

I have, actually. And you understand, don't you, that I'm not going to bring home a guy who articles for me and fuck him in our bed.

He climbed the stairs shaking. At the top, he started to go back down to the car for his stuff, and then he remembered he'd left everything at the retreat.

She had closed up downstairs and followed him up. Where are your bags? she said.

I just took off.

After they beat you up.

He touched his cheekbone. Winced. You mean this? I slipped, getting my pillow.

You slipped getting your pillow.

It was interesting, but eight days was enough.

You've been gone nine.

Nine days. How was the spa?

Fabulous.

You came back early.

No, you did. I was always coming back today. You never listen.

LAPSANG SOUCHONG

Once there was a man named Booth who had so little psychology, who was so innocent of the difference between how
he saw things and how they were, that he might as well have
been an American. But when he applied for a green card,
the US Immigration Service required of his wife a hundred-
page essay proving that she and Booth had a relationship,
and she got stuck on page three. In the end Booth hired a
ghostwriter, who cobbled together enough shared moments
from her life with her boyfriend to qualify Booth for a card.
But if US Immigration was satisfied, the seed of doubt had
been planted in the mind of Booth's wife, who worried that
if Booth loved her it was not because he found her shortcomings endearing, or because they didn't matter to him
one way or the other, but because he had no idea what they

were, and once they became obvious to him, he would treat them as if they didn't exist, and yet nothing would be the same again.

The marriage lasted six months.

Booth could be as interested in the next person as the next person, but it depended on who that was. In his view there were good guys and bad guys, and he didn't want to know any more about the bad guys than it would take him to be sure that that's what they were. The truth is, bad guys have every reason to pass as good guys, if they can. Also, nobody's perfect. Much of Booth's energy, which otherwise might have gone into taking an interest in what was going on for himself and by the same token for the next person, went into figuring out who was a good guy and who was not. It wasn't easy. Booth's wife, for example, had shown every sign of being a good guy, but when she asked for a divorce, Booth was amazed to discover that this was not remotely the case. Fortunately, righteous anger is a good-guy emotion — unlike disappointment, say, or feeling like a failure. Also, he already had his green card.

Like a newscaster's speech impediment, a psychology-free approach to human behaviour can be career-determining. Soon Booth was writing long-form profiles of rich and famous people for large-circulation US magazines and weekend supplements, where the psychology is off-the-rack and the good guy/bad guy question is in the air but not on the page. In a land where everybody can achieve their dream if they try hard enough, it's more about success and failure, and nobody understands anything until the story ends.

‹ ‹ ‹

On a sunny weekday morning in early September, Sally
Dowbiggin was watering her plants in the sunroom of her
home in Santa Barbara when the doorbell rang. This would
be the man from the magazine.

Mrs. Dowbiggin — ?

Maybe it was the earnest affect or something unconvinc-
ing about the crumpled linen jacket and the spiked hair, but
Sally Dowbiggin's first words — not happy — were,

They've sent a Canadian.

I'm working on that, Booth wisecracked as she led him
through the house. And it's *aboot* time.

In the sunroom, she invited him to take a seat, Roger
would be down in a minute. But Booth had no way to know
which chair was Roger Dowbiggin's. The panic in his eyes
conveyed this, but all Sally Dowbiggin said was,

Any one.

Booth chose a chair that in ten minutes would be full in
the sun.

You like sun? she said.

He blinked up at her. The skin under his eyes was twitching in what was already dazzling brightness. I'm fine, he
said. When she just looked at him, he got up and moved to
Roger Dowbiggin's favourite chair.

She offered him tea or coffee, unless he'd prefer something cold.

Tea would be great, he said, still rattled. Lapsang
Souchong, if you've got.

I don't.

No problem. In that case anything'll do.

She looked at him.

Really. It's fine. I'm easy. Anything.

As she got her keys from the front hall, she wondered if this one had a mind. In her experience, Canadians were more likely to have a mind. The ones who didn't probably stayed home. But Canadians didn't understand anything, they got things as wrong as anybody else, just different things, which didn't mean that what this one wrote wouldn't make a slick, magaziney sort of sense or that bits and pieces wouldn't wash up in articles stretching all the way to the *Times* obituary, which would be a Googledump of half-truths and misattributions by a staffer who wasn't born when Roger Dowbiggin changed television forever.

At the Whole Foods she found Lapsang Souchong and then she drove back.

‹ ‹ ‹

Roger Dowbiggin had heard the doorbell and he heard Sally take the hall from the sunroom. He heard voices but not the words. A few minutes later he heard the car in the driveway and thought *Uh-oh*.

For months Roger had been waking with a vague sense of implication in a questionable act. As usual, he'd engaged in it in a state of mental blindness, and afterward he'd pushed it so far out of his mind that he couldn't remember what it was or if it had actually happened and who else was involved, because there was always somebody else involved. It was like an occasional sexual thing with a male friend, when they drank, neither of them able to admit to himself that it kept happening, that it wasn't just the one time. Like a sleepwalker, he'd been having sex every few years with his old buddy, and what was that about? Or it was not remembering until he'd just taken acid that he'd taken it twice this week already. Or a shoplifting penchant. He'd come in the door with his coat weighted down with items he had no need for and no memory of pocketing.

But this morning when he woke up and saw the date, he knew what it was: he'd agreed to another profile. He had a reason, the new show. But still. Fuck.

‹ ‹ ‹

As Booth waited for Sally Dowbiggin to bring him something to drink (why had he said Lapsang Souchong? he hated Lapsang Souchong, it tasted like hot pine-tar water) he thought about how Parisian women keep themselves beautifully together even into old age, as tight and flirtatious as when they were twenty, so the male desire to be on hand when passion blows the package wide open can remain intact. Sally Dowbiggin didn't seem to be Parisian, or even French, but she made Booth want to be there when passion blew her wide open, and thinking this, he reflected how far his ex-wife had been from having this effect on him, probably because she was an uncomplicated sort of woman and yet, unaccountably, rotten to the core.

She's given you nothing to drink, Roger Dowbiggin said from the doorway. He seemed amused by this apparent oversight.

It's all right! Booth exclaimed, leaping to his feet. She — Where'd she go? Sit. *Sit.*

Booth sat.

So did Roger Dowbiggin, in a chair kitty-corner to his usual, which the journalist had taken for himself.

‹ ‹ ‹

Bacteria have a quorum-sensing ability. They release molecules that let them know when a critical mass has been reached and it's time to turn on the virulence genes. By then it can be too late for the host. It's the same with journalists. The quorum they're waiting to sense is the reader disapproval numbers for a particular individual, and as soon as the critical mass is reached, they turn on the virulence. When working on a story, Booth put aside his good guy/bad guy thinking, but like any good journalist he possessed a quorum-sensing ability, and from the moment Roger Dowbiggin appeared in the sunroom doorway, this ability told Booth that he could turn on the virulence at any time. What exactly it was, Booth couldn't have said. The way Dowbiggin immediately blamed his wife when he saw his visitor had nothing to drink? The pleasure he seemed to take in giving people nasty starts? The two-hundred-dollar haircut, the silk dressing gown? Something. It didn't matter. Booth had been around. He knew what these big shots were like. How these things tended to go.

‹ ‹ ‹

Roger Dowbiggin had made his first hundred million in real estate and before that in cable television, as a producer of quiz and reality shows, most notably *Now, That's Just Plain*

Stupid! and *Why, That's Positively Grotesque!* His new show, his first in five years, premiering in the fall, *I Can't Believe I'm Watching This!*, was the hook for Booth's piece. But Roger had already been casting around for a new project, starting last year with negotiations with the inventor of StyroCon, interlocking concrete blocks that were light, strong, and superior insulators because they were filled with hard-shelled Styrofoam pellets. Also, unlike drywall, StyroCon remained unaffected by flooding and so was well suited for the coming times. Homes could be built where they couldn't be built even now. But when the Mob wanted 50 percent of the American rights just to allow StyroCon a Rhode Island tryout, Roger walked.

Next he'd looked into Internet porn, where the rank amateurs were doing the best work. Watching people of all ages, genders, races, and body types having sex with themselves and others, he experienced warm upsurges of solidarity with his fellow human creatures and was moved by the ardour of the most ordinary and unassuming when they found themselves in front of a camera with no clothes on or every intention of removing them. Where did they get their ideas? How did they know he'd enjoy watching them do that? You could call this vanity or exhibitionism or the follies of arousal, but the effect was more like an invitation to a private moment that could be anybody's private moment. Are we all the same, then? Young, old? Male, female, TG? Are there body-mischief universals?

Who could have predicted the power of ubiquitous porn to illuminate in the human imagination the human body in its radical simplicity and bracing absence of clutter? Who would have guessed that with fake passion the coin of the realm, the real thing would remain the one true currency? Who would have guessed that if you really want erotic, you need a frame, some indication of who these people are and how they have come to be in this outrageous, lust-maddened state? Who would have guessed that symptoms of another person's arousal could be as contagious as the yawn of a stranger on the subway?

Roger remembered once hearing a priest chastise the young woman who would throw away her life for one night of passion and on the same day reading Henry Miller on a Clichy whore who was no more capable of experiencing passion than of producing a diamond. And now Roger marvelled that in a single bound, passion, historically at the same time aggrandized and diminished by invested claims, had broken free of the priests and the streets and the marriage bed together, with no terrible price to be paid by anybody. It was a virtual miracle, a secular absolution. Unfortunately, with so many so willing to give so much to so many for so little — not even passing fame, the faces refused to stay in the mind, none of it stayed in the mind — and consequently, along with no price to be paid, no money to be made, Roger understood that these were the salad days of Internet porn. Soon it would be back to gatekeeping and fees, to the bimbos and the jimbos, to showbiz and fake passion, and who in their right mind wanted solidarity with that?

Roger's porn research had got him thinking once more about television, where interesting things had been happening again. But how do you follow a guaranteed barnburner like *I Can't Believe I'm Watching This!*? Presumably, as porn has, you cut back to something more authentic, because, what do you know, it's better! It's not a high pixel count that turns a screen into a window.

As he answered Booth's questions — while watching Booth's eyes shift between his notes and a point somewhere over his (Roger's) left shoulder and Booth's face muscles arrange and rearrange themselves in expressions intended to convey interest, reflection, amusement, and so on — Roger's mind's eye rose like a camera on a winch, to the ceiling. From there it watched his hand reach out toward the side table for Sally's soil-moisture metre, which he would plunge into Booth's eyes. First the right, then the left.

Roger didn't do this, but then he nearly did it anyway, in order to do something that would not relate to anything. It wouldn't be something he wanted to do, but neither would it be the last thing he wanted to do. It would be more than unconsidered, or inadvisable, it would be senseless.

When he also didn't do it anyway, Roger immediately regretted this. At the same time, he was relieved that he didn't, because that would have meant willing it, and willed, it wouldn't have been senseless but to make a point. The point was that the searchlight such an act would cause to shine back down through the years of his life, illuminating some things and darkening others *and thereby changing the meaning of everything that had come before this one act*, was only the sort of thing that minds do. Whereas putting out the interviewer's eyes would need to be unrelated to anything. An act committed for no reason at all. That way, no matter how much anybody knew or found out about Roger Dowbiggin, no matter how compelling the theories they came up with for why on earth he would do such a thing, he alone would know how wrong they were. It would make no difference what they thought they knew, how authoritative they came across as, or how many people their specious arguments convinced.

But *would* he know? Or would he be the first to go rooting back through his life for signs and portents that one day he would do something like this? Because surely anybody with his wits about him must have seen it coming, and whose wits could be more about him than his own?

Let's talk about the new show, Booth was saying. You've described it as a radical departure. How so?

But even as Booth said these words, he was looking toward the door. When Roger looked too, he saw Sally, with a tray, starting for the side table, which he reached for, to clear away a few magazines and the soil-moisture metre.

Don't let me interrupt, Sally said.

‹ ‹ ‹

How old is she? Booth asked himself as he watched Sally Dowbiggin cross the room toward him. If she's fifty, she looks thirty-five. Or maybe thirty-eight, or forty. More important, how old does she look when she's blown wide open? She was carrying the tray like a priestess conveying a sacrament, or dynamite. He wondered what kind of tea it was, and why it had taken her so long. As she set the tray on the side table, Gunpowder? Booth joked, enigmatically.

Lapsang Souchong, Sally said. What you asked for.

You found some! Excellent!

We were just talking about the new show, Dowbiggin said.

I can't believe you were doing that, Sally said, pouring Booth's tea. Nobody else was having any.

Booth laughed immoderately. He couldn't understand the Lapsang Souchong.

Dowbiggin held up the soil-moisture metre. I was thinking of plunging this into his eyes. First the right, then the left.

Let me get the camera, Sally said.

But then what? Dowbiggin said. Pundits sitting behind a desk pronouncing on an act that none of them understands and nobody watching should be expecting them to? Experts advancing ideas that are more about them, hanging out their shingles, when in fact nobody knows anything? But on they talk, and the hours fill and the days pass?

That would be television, Sally said.

If it worked at all it would only work for him, Dowbiggin said, indicating Booth. He's the only one who wouldn't be so sure any more he knows what's coming.

Sally looked at Booth. Roger thinks people need to stop being so sure.

This isn't about me, Dowbiggin said. It's about human nature.

‹ ‹ ‹

As a working journalist, Booth was no stranger to face-tiousness or contempt. What he couldn't understand was how purportedly intelligent people could fail to grasp that all it took was an adjective here, a verb there. They seemed to assume he'd do his worst anyway, so what the hell. Sometimes he wondered if only a bad guy would ever consent to a magazine profile of himself because only a bad guy could be sufficiently attracted to the challenge of keeping his true nature hidden to be willing to submit to the sort of in-depth scrutiny he'll receive from a tough-minded professional like Booth.

To sight! Booth joked. Mine! and offered a Lapsang Souchong toast that failed to elicit a response. Sally was on her way out the door. Dowbiggin was watching her go.

Booth took a gulp of the tea — it was just awful, a scalding infusion of smoked conifer — and repeated his question about the new show, which Dowbiggin failed to answer while contemplatively turning the soil-moisture metre in his hands.

Okay, Dowbiggin said. We know the entire history of the universe is pouring into every instant of the existence of everything. But what does this mean? Suddenly I do something bizarre, and everybody, including me, behaves as though with enough information it could have been predicted. What is this confidence in information we don't, and can't, have? How do you encourage people to appreciate that anything can happen at any time and the ones who say they saw it coming are delusional, opportunists, or liars?

Here Dowbiggin stopped asking questions and looked at Booth. When Booth didn't say anything, he gave him a hint. Weekly, say, and once we're in reruns, daily.

Television? Booth said. He didn't believe this for a second, of course, nobody would, and he wondered what on earth had Dowbiggin thinking he could play him for a fool. With a thin smile he asked if it was this line of thinking that had led to the creation of *I Can't Believe I'm Watching This!*

Dowbiggin didn't seem to hear the question. He was leaning forward with his head tilted as if to speak directly into Booth's ear. The new show, Dowbiggin said. Not this one. The next. Vulnerability. Tenacity of a tentative kind. Humility. Maybe you'll be in it. Maybe I will. Maybe we'll call it *Hellzacomin!* It's a new age, Mr. Booth. Dowbiggin Productions brought us here, and now we're back, to push us through to the other side.

‹ ‹ ‹

In the kitchen, Sally wondered how long the Canadian had been planning to stay. She'd assumed that whoever they sent would stay for lunch. But not this one. She looked at her watch. In half an hour, lunch for this one would be out of the question.

‹ ‹ ‹

Booth put a hand to his eyes.

Are you all right? Dowbiggin said.

Feeling a little strange.

That'd be Sally. You drank up all your tea? Good. Let me help you to your car. You'll want to be on the road while you can still drive.

After Sally gave Booth a hand with what he assumed was his hat, though as far as he knew he hadn't worn one, they helped him to his car and stood on the slate driveway in front of the house, Dowbiggin with his hands in the pockets of his silk gown, Sally at his side.

‹ ‹ ‹

Although Booth understood that he was sitting behind the wheel of his own car, he couldn't think what he was supposed to do next, especially with both Dowbiggins standing right there. When he looked again, Sally had an arm around her husband, though for a moment Booth wasn't sure which of them — himself or Dowbiggin — her arm was actually around. And then she disappeared. When she rapped at his window, he jumped. He couldn't get it open, so he opened the door.

Just checking it's turned on, she said.

What?

As he looked at her, she fiddled with the thing on his forehead. He put his hand to it and to the strap that held it there. It felt like a headlamp.

Careful, Sally said. It's practically indestructible, but you don't want to smear the lens. By the way, there's a mic, so don't hesitate to sigh or whistle or make odd sounds or talk to yourself. We want to be right here with you.

She was looking at him.

You'll need your key, she said.

He held out his hand.

No. In your pocket.

When he found a whole set of them, he thought they must be for the thing on his head, but she was indicating a slot in the dashboard.

In there, she said.

He inserted one of the keys, intrigued that his hand would know which one.

Now turn it, she said.

He turned the key. The engine started.

She closed the door. Remember, she said through the glass. Speed kills.

Booth pulled away. It was like a miracle.

In the rear-view, Sally Dowbiggin waved. Dowbiggin himself, with his hands still in the pockets of his silk gown, just stood watching him go. As Booth waved, he feared that they wouldn't be able to see his hand for the reflection in the back window, so he opened his door and held out his arm, low down, with the hand back-turned, to display the palm, waggling it a little to let them know that, yes, he'd felt indisposed and had to make a hasty exit but he was fine now and things were already coming together with the profile.

When he closed his door, his attention turned to the scene ahead, and it was one of those absolutely gorgeous days, the kind that lights up the screen when you're flipping. It was also like a video game, or maybe that's just how things seem when cars are coming at you when you have a camera on your head. They were peeling away to the left and right, some on two wheels practically, their drivers waving and shouting out their windows what sounded like furious or perhaps only alarmed greetings. He didn't know how to get his window down and couldn't hear them. He opened his door again, but he was going too fast now, as fast as they were, easily, and the wind was too loud. When he closed his door, it came to him — and this was something he knew right away he'd use in the article, because the thing about a writer, he's always working. Leaving the Dowbiggins' was like driving at high speed onto a Roger Dowbiggin set, with everybody careening right and left when they weren't about to break into song or into a big dance number that has the whole world rushing and elbowing into the frame, and all the while you're watching this, you know that something even crazier is coming. Unconscionably crazy. Yes, he would use this, it was perfect, he would call it "Roger Dowbiggin's Secret Weapon," because it was obvious the key to the story was Sally Dowbiggin, your tight package that all of a sudden blows wide open, and nothing is the same again.

THE AMAZING INSULT

Gretta had been with Chris since she was fifteen and didn't know much about relationships beyond what she'd had with him, not first-hand anyway, but what she'd had with him was okay, normal, she supposed, real life, though at some point she stopped having a lot to say to him and maybe she never did, and after twenty-two years and with the kids grown up and moved out, Chris was mostly focused on his career, which was understandable and had paid off. For him the sailboat was an apogee of personal success, but the first summer they had it out on the water they ran into a sudden storm that thirty years ago would have been called freak but was now common, and the boom swung round and dealt Gretta such a blow to the head that from that moment on she was excused from all that, and when she changed, every-thing changed.

Chris himself became so strange to her that you would think the boom had struck him too. With Gretta no longer herself, he accused her of affairs and then had one him-self, and when, in an unrelated development, she did too, in his rage when he found out (because when he asked her point-blank she answered point-blank, being disinclined, in consequence of that blow, to lie, ever again) he spent the better part of a Sunday going through the house destroy-ing all signs of the person she had been, using a razor to cut her out of photographs and a Magic Marker to black her out of his journals. For her this meant the loss of any outward trace of her former self. By his actions she had been cut adrift and now would need to make a fresh start in the world.

Chris initiated divorce proceedings, she sued, they settled. She rented a bachelor apartment and got a job in an office. There were other changes. The blow left her susceptible to blindsides by horniness. A word that kept coming to mind, one her mother had used for certain women, a word Gretta had always hated, was *oversexed*. She would walk around thinking, What is the *matter* with me? and then think, Oh right, I'm horny. The affair had been an unfortunate side effect of that. Just how unfortunate she didn't understand until her lover reached over to brush the hair from her eyes and she recoiled from such intimacy.

Gretta was now also super smart. Her brain was firing on eight cylinders instead of the former six at the best of times and most of the time four. The world now arrayed before her was stranger, more complex, more promising.

Remarkably, her new perceptions had no quality of mania or paranoia about them, just morning clarity. More often than not she got things right and certainly had no need of a Chris for that.

The risk in being new to everything — now that a lie felt like a refusal, like a shovelful of clay landing on a coffin with her inside it having a fit — was drawing too much attention to herself. Ordinary social interaction runs on dedicated tracks, and it doesn't take much before people are giving you looks. But most of the looks are so unthinking she wondered how conscious they could be. Another thing she started to notice was how good people are at accommodating unexpected responses. Mainly they do it by not listening.

Nice day, they'd say, and the weather guy claimed it would rain all weekend.

And she'd say, Beautiful. This morning I saw five or six robins in one bush. Are robins *flocking* now?

One of those looks, and then: Yeah — Half the time these jokers have no idea.

People didn't need to think about it, they made the necessary adjustments and said what they'd intended to say. Gretta now thought of ideas as machines of the air, puppeteer overlords. Fortunately, an eight-cylinder brain goes its own way, to the twangs of stretching and snapping strings.

Now when she went out she thought of herself as taking her brain along, to see what it made of things. When visiting the home of people she didn't know, on a shelf or a mantelpiece she would leave a framed photograph of herself. She knew this was an odd thing to do. It went against her inclination, but going against her inclination was something she was now inclined to do. When you don't go along, you keep running into the steely constrictions of what you've stopped going along with. On the other hand, behave even a little differently and doors open you never knew existed. So she didn't worry about it. This is how she treated her behaviour in general. It doesn't take much to be off track, but when people don't listen you have all this leeway. They didn't warm to her as one of their own, but who wants to be warmed to by people who don't listen?

Before the storm blew in and the boom swung round, she'd assumed people naturally cared more than she now knew they did. That had been generous of her, she supposed, but it had had her counting on others when she should have been counting on herself. Now, instead of worrying about not fitting in, she paid attention to what was going on around her and what she was doing with it. She was often surprised but never bothered by what she saw or did. It was all new, it was all strange. It all mattered. And for the first time she understood the importance of not allowing anybody a greater stake than she had in where things were going for her.

Some people have multiple selves. When a situation calls for a self with more experience dealing with this sort of thing, it takes over. Often the selves know each other only by hearsay or from mysterious bruises or finding ticket stubs in their purse from events they don't remember attending. Sometimes the selves can be so different from each other that they require different-strength glasses, suffer different allergies, even have different-coloured eyes. Gretta had just the two selves, first the one and then the other, and the second remembered the first as well as anybody remembers an earlier stage in their life, and with the same amusement and dismay. But also like most people Gretta tended to under-estimate how much she had understood before. Chris kept a journal because he envied hers, though when he started she stopped, but not before she'd learned how long ideas she tended to think were new with her had been on her mind, sometimes since her teens or childhood. Not so well expressed when they first showed up, but the same ideas.

At the same time, Gretta really was somebody else now and still finding out what kind of person that was. She had just turned forty-one, but the relative inexperience of her new self had her feeling like eighteen again, without the mood swings. That, and the heightened intelligence, and the frequency of her surprise at things and at her responses to them, and the nagging horniness. A word aside from *over-sexed* that kept coming to mind was *experience*, which to her and her friends when they were teenagers had meant sexual experience, as in (spoken as if sympathetically) *She hasn't had any experience*. That's how Gretta thought of herself now, as one who hadn't had any *experience*, except experience not in the sense of what as adolescents they used to call *doing dirties* but physical and emotional intimacy with another person. What she'd had with Chris, except she was pretty sure that had she been the person then she was now, what she'd had with Chris would not have been enough.

Life was strange, but it must have always been. It wasn't just the novelty, it was how things were.

‹ ‹ ‹

One night before leaving a party that was just getting started, Gretta was placing a picture of herself amidst a half-dozen others on the dresser in the bedroom where the coats were piled when she noticed a black-and-white photograph of a girl fourteen or fifteen, on a beach, in a one-piece bathing suit, standing a little awkwardly, one leg positioned in front of the other, with a child slumped over in the sand next to her — a tall, lonely, responsible young woman gazing soberly into the camera — and she fell in love.

Who is this? she asked Ellen, who was in the kitchen peering into an oven at a tray of hors d'oeuvres.

It's me, your host, Ellen said, but when she turned and saw the picture she said, Oh. My sister Frances. This is us at Wasaga. She pointed to the baby. That's me. Out of it, as usual. Frances is older. More your age. Not that that's old.

Where is she?

Ottawa.

Can I meet her?

Sure, Ellen said. And then she said, Why?

She looks like an interesting person.

You mean not like semi-collapsed little baby me?

I hardly know you, Gretta said. I'm sure you're wild, and they both laughed, but Gretta worried that she'd played into a deflection and would never meet Frances. She couldn't ask Ellen for her sister's contact information, because that would be even stranger than asking to meet her on the basis of a twenty-five-year-old photograph, and so she said,

Promise you'll tell me when she's in town next, and I'll have you both over.

Okay, Ellen said quickly. But right now you'll have to excuse me while I char all the grease I can out of these fuckers —

This was another deflection.

I'm going to hold you to it, Gretta said.

Hold away, Ellen said, opening the oven again. And then she looked round at Gretta and added, more kindly, Consider me held.

Gretta put the picture of Ellen's sister back on the dresser, next to the one of herself, and left the party. She understood that placing Ellen's sister's picture next to hers was even stranger than leaving a picture of herself in the first place. Why, given this sudden escalation of the stakes, was she pushing her luck? But what the hell. Was Ellen the sort to be easily spooked? Also, there would be everything about her sister that she knew and Gretta didn't, which could make introducing her to a person like Gretta, especially the new and improved Gretta, something Ellen would want to do, once she'd had a chance to think about it. Or maybe she hadn't needed to think about it, and that's why she'd told Gretta to consider her held. Why couldn't this interest be a godsend, a chance to get her sister out of a rut, or a fix? Nothing's easier than painting yourself into a corner, especially for a woman, as she attempts to please too many other people. Sometimes the right input, the right jog, can be all it takes. Why should Gretta even be going into this worrying it was inadvisable? Who could say for sure what it was? Maybe the strangeness was that she felt so certain. It doesn't take much to leave the rails — a tap on the wheel, a blow to the head — but once you do, it's all uncharted territory.

When Gretta woke up the next morning with the girl in the photograph very much on her mind, she resolved not to hound Ellen or to worry about her not coming through. Nothing would be achieved by behaving like a crazy person.

An awareness that some of your behaviour is a little odd is not a licence to go hog-wild. And it wasn't as if she knew anything about what Frances would be like a quarter century after somebody took a picture of her on a beach. Maybe her sister should have a say in whether anything would, or could, happen. Still, for Gretta it was hard waiting and not knowing, when she felt so sure.

But not two weeks later Ellen called to say that Frances was coming to town for a conference the weekend after next and would be happy to meet her.

So come for dinner, Gretta said. Which night?

‹ ‹ ‹

It was just the three of them. As Frances followed her sister in the door, unselfconsciously looking around, taking it all in, Gretta knew that the difficulty would be remembering that this woman did not know her, it would be assuming intimacy on insufficient grounds and thus failing to put her most important guest, ever, at ease enough to have any hope of seeing her again.

At first Frances was reserved the way anyone first in the home of a stranger who has mysteriously expressed interest in her would be reserved. But once she realized that Gretta was not a nut she relaxed, and soon she was making them all laugh by putting on a show of being repeatedly taken aback by Ellen's right-wing thinking since her second marriage, to a businessman, a tendency that Ellen played up for the occasion. Ellen would say that of course decreasing taxes on the rich is good for everybody, and Frances would gaze at her dolefully and say, I can't begin to express how misguided I think that is, and they would all laugh, and Gretta wanted nothing more than that one day Frances would gaze at her dolefully and say, I can't begin to express how misguided I think that is.

As they were leaving, Gretta could tell that for Ellen the evening had fallen within the parameters of a normal dinner party, considering. As for Frances, she was as friendly as she'd been since she'd understood that Gretta was not a nut, but she wasn't exactly behaving like a woman swept off her feet, which of course recommended her even more. The most accurate construction on the evening that Gretta could come up with was that it had gone all right but was a little disappointing.

The next day she left a message for Frances at her hotel, and when Frances returned her call, Gretta asked if they could meet for coffee, which they did later that afternoon in the restaurant off the lobby, with Frances's bags piled next to the table, because she had already checked out and had her flight back to Ottawa to catch.

Gretta told her she thought she was great.

Thank you, Frances said. And then she said, You know I'm married.

I don't think I'm talking about jumping into bed, Gretta said.

So friendship, Frances said. Not too soon there, possibly?

And they both laughed.

But most people are unhappy in their relationship, and while at any particular time they can't be budged, there will come a time when they can. The difficulty is not betraying impatience, and the best way to do that is by not being impatient. The difficulty is remaining available without seeming to hover. Gretta and Frances had talked about friendship because they didn't really know each other and neither of them had ever been with a woman, but once the sex happened, which it did three and a half months later, the next time Frances was in Toronto, it was so transfiguring — Gretta's instinct, if that's what it was, had been dead-on; *It's sweet you've got such a filthy mind*, Frances told her at one point, before she came again — that there was no question, and within a year Frances had found a job in Toronto, they bought a condo, and even with the transition from fantasy to real life, everything was good, which is to say it was better than good.

‹ ‹ ‹

Like all new relationships, and like Gretta herself, it was a new world. Frances was not another Chris. She was as smart as he was, but in a way that reminded Gretta that in Chris, long before she'd met him, something had shut down, although until now she'd assumed that everybody would seem this way once you got to know them or never quite did. People at close quarters are a shuffle of closed doors, she'd always imagined, nobody ever really gets to know anybody, we're as mysterious to each other as we are to ourselves, and so on. And then there are those who are just plain thrown by being loved, who prefer to limit the exchange to being seen and heard. Clothed, naked, with legs, with cheeks, spread, it didn't matter, but not loved. Anything but being loved. It's too real, it expects too much of them, they don't deserve it, they're imposters, they'll lose it because of who they actually are, what they secretly feel. It's a kind of hopelessness about themselves. A timorous, stubborn despair.

This was not Frances, who had no problem with being loved. Which she was, at last, as much surely as anybody ever could be, by Gretta, for whom the thing about loving Frances, at first anyway, was that, unlike Chris's, Frances's behaviour was not a problem that needed to be worked around or solved. One reason for this was that Gretta's desire for her was one thing, the other was her love for who this person was. To love this woman solely for her beauty or her charm, her innumerable charms, was for somebody on the rails. Gretta had left the rails. Frances for Gretta was like what models in magazines were for her now. She saw the image, and under it, under the makeup, under the attitude, under the look — in the case of the model, of imperious indifference, in the case of Frances, of a kind of sombre bemusement — she saw the reality of an arrested child or an avaricious dullard or a skittery little creature or a sweet soul. You see past the image created by your desire and you see the person. The face behind the face. Gretta didn't, at first, feel baffled or stymied by an image she had of Frances or that Frances had of herself. And what did Gretta see past her image of Frances? Lawless innocence. The same thing she'd seen past the image of that young girl on the beach, posing awkwardly for the camera. Greta was in love with that. If she lusted for the girl, now a woman, it was the person she loved. The lawless innocent.

But people up close can be surprising, and in nothing so much as how little they value what you find most precious in them. Their sights are on other matters, matters that have absorbed them since long before you loved them. This can be disconcerting, and at first you can't believe they're serious. You think, This is them from before, they won't go on like this (now that they have me). But of course they do. Your love has affirmed them. Small signs turn out to be symptoms of undeniable, intractable, worrisome behaviours. People say you can't judge a book by its cover, but it's all there. The trick is knowing the difference between what you hope will be inside and what the cover is clearly telling you is inside.

‹ ‹ ‹

Frances was a lawyer. Her new job was with an international non-profit that tracked and publicized global warming, and the reality of those statistics and that fight became a major part of her and Gretta's lives. Spend time and take an interest, and like dough in a warming oven the subject of your concern will swell. To Gretta it made sense that Frances would be attracted to this kind of work, and that even with people being people and every powerful corporation and government on earth preferring to do nothing when not being actively obstructive, she would not approach it with a negative attitude. You do this kind of work because you need an income and have the skills and care about the earth and take satisfaction in defying institutional power. When Frances came home each night no less optimistic than the night before, Gretta thought of her as an actress, still in the role, so it was a shock when she realized she was serious. To hear Frances, her colleagues were pure of heart and free of personal ambition, the nations of the world would come together because it was the right thing to do, science would find a way, and the earth would be fixed.

The old Gretta had mostly read magazines. Now it was books, every chance she could get, and when she read about climate change she despaired, and when she read that the self is a function of a childlike belief that we will not be harmed, she thought of Frances, who was fearless and undefended, who still believed. This made Gretta feel cynical and defeatist and also like the adult in the relationship, and if she could have taken Frances's hand and walked her away from all error and harm, she would have. Instead, her behaviour shifted, in ways invisible to herself but not to Frances, who may have been childlike in some ways but was not a fool.

Why have you started behaving like a man? Frances asked her one day.

What?

Something's bothering me, and I try to talk to you about it, and you're right there with reasons why I feel like this and what I should do about it. You seem to think anything that bothers me is a problem I expect you to solve. As if I'm always a little bit sick and you have the remedy. This is how men think. Can't you understand that all I need you to do is *listen*?

I do listen, Gretta said, but this was what Chris used to say. He could listen, but he couldn't stop there. So had she become him, her lost spouse, treating hers now like a child, assuming she knew what Frances should do to be happy and safe, as opposed to a fool or a sitting duck, because she feared Frances was like her own former self, with no idea how the world worked and what it was capable of?

I'm a grown woman, Frances would remind her.

But it kept happening. Gretta thought of people as becoming adults when they've sustained just the right amount of damage to convince them that with strong-enough defences they can stop it from happening again, and that damage and those defences are who they are. Too much damage and people's defences break down. Too little and they aren't adults yet. Frances had either sustained too little damage or failed to take it on, and while innocence may be its own defence, Gretta doubted it. Her fear was that Frances needed protection from nothing so much as Gretta herself. Gretta feared the blow had caused her to lose, along with the ability to lie, a feel for healthy boundaries. The lawless innocence she'd glimpsed in the picture of the girl on the beach had been a promise that these boundaries would somehow not apply. But it turned out they did. The innocence required it. And yet while Gretta could feel the seduction of the old boundaries, of keeping her own counsel, she couldn't seem to do that, possibly because she feared becoming again the person who in twenty-two years had rarely told her spouse what she actually thought, about anything.

You're going to have to let me make my own mistakes, Frances would warn her.

I don't want you hurt, that's all.

That's *all*? You're sure? I can't be *hurt*?

And Gretta would wake in the night afraid she'd been over-impressed by her own boldness, when in fact it had been too easy, because Frances lacked sense, and anybody else would have seen that. Other times — and this was terrible — she was afraid it was like buying something and being thrilled with it and with the price you paid and then gradually discovering what was wrong with it and why it hadn't been such a bargain after all. In fact you were fleeced. Other times Gretta would think that we all have our blind spots and shortcomings, and this is why you give people the benefit of the doubt. You have no idea what handicaps they labour under. Try being a landlord if you want to know the chaos of most people's lives and their hapless, hit-and-miss ways of finding and asserting order. Get to know almost anybody and you'll catch glimpses of a lifetime of bad judgement and wasted time — an appalling amount of wasted time — and you'll come up against pain and fear and suffering and a hundred strategies for avoiding all of it. Gretta knew this, she'd known it before, but this new life was hers too, a gift, a second chance, and like anybody starting out, she was reluctant to compromise.

Frances would say, If you love me you'll let me be me.

And Gretta would think, But what if your naïveté confounds me? What if I feel I have to silence myself around you? What if I doubt the quality of your discernment in all things, including your love for me? What if the world is more complicated than you seem to understand? What if *I* am? And she would tell herself she was being neurotic and anybody would need time to adjust to a happy relationship after twenty-two years in an unhappy one. And she would wonder if Frances could change, and if she could, why she would want to when she felt she was being judged and criticized. Who except a patient on a table or a couch or a woman over her head in love with a man would be crazy enough to let in somebody intent on *fixing* her? It's a tricky word, *fix*, the way it can jump around from *make right* to *stabilize* to *deprive of flow* to *punish* to *silence* to *terminate*.

This must have been why they could have been arguing about themselves when they argued about the amazing insult to the earth known as global warming. And why when one day Gretta said in exasperation, *Come on, Fran, grow up, the earth isn't fixable, the people who aren't working for themselves are working for a salary*, Frances leaned toward her and said, *But if the earth's not fixable, then this isn't, because your love is poison to me*, and the next day she was gone.

THE FORCE OF THE WORLD

On party nights Nick's parents would climb the stairs with their drinks and descend an hour later like movie stars, wisecracking and smelling of alcohol and White Shoulders. Wolf would put on Mart Kenney or Artie Shaw and they'd dance. Sometimes they looked so glamorous that Nick, who wanted something for when they were not like this, would beg them to let him take their picture. By the time the three of them left the house, Wolf would be saucer-eyed from the rye and gingers, like a man continuing to discover with delight and amazement developments of stupendous import, Josephine would be plucking invisible lint from her top, the way she did when she knew people were looking at her, and Nick would be floating.

On the night of Hurricane Hazel, the party was at the Kembleys', at the top of the street. Joe Kembley was Wolf's boss at Kembley Cotton, but it was a small town. By the time Nick and his parents arrived, the kids had locked themselves in the Kembleys' bedroom and refused to let him in. He could hear them fighting in there over who would wear what. Instead of telling, he walked down the hall to Bobby Kembley's room and climbed out Bobby's window and edged along the roof with his heels in the eavestrough. Out in the night again, he could feel the wind stronger than when he had left the house with his parents. There was also now a stinging rain. He was looking out over the Humber Valley, but the night was black, he could have been anywhere. The Kembleys' bedroom window wasn't locked. He got the sash up and climbed in and pushed through kids trying on the Kembleys' stuff, to Dora Kembley's closet, where Bobby was flicking through his mother's tops.

Why are you wet? Bobby said.

The kids' fashion show that night had the adults shifting in their seats. Nick couldn't tell if it was because some of the kids had got into Dora Kembley's underwear or it was something else. He thought they'd done it now, but when it was over, the audience roared to its feet like one great animal, and he understood that every wardrobe decision and backstage wrangle had been critical to the night's excellence. Normally the inanity of applause had him casting around for something to destroy. But that night it erupted from adults so flushed with sympathy and delight that he simply dropped from the waist and let the adulation roll through him. Afterward, with Bobby *yaying* in the lead, they ran back upstairs to throw together an encore. But their moment had passed. They were careless now with triumph and exhaustion. Already they had forgotten how much had gone into their initial success. They could not knuckle down. After fifteen minutes, to rancorous objections, with his usual charm, to everybody's secret relief, Bobby pulled the plug, they would watch TV, and they used up the last of their energy fighting to be the last one on the Kembleys' bed. Eventually they calmed down and fell asleep in front of *Flying Down to Rio*.

‹ ‹ ‹

Later, when Nick reached for his blankie and got a handful of scarves, he knew he was back in Dora Kembley's closet. When he crawled out, the storm was louder. All the kids had gone home. There was only Bobby, asleep on his parents' bed, still wearing one of Dora's tops. Nick's own clothes were scattered around the room. He climbed out of his fashion show gear, which was mostly Joe Kembley's, and put his own clothes back on — his sweater must have shrunk in the rain — along with his father's fedora, which he'd worn in the show, and went downstairs. There he found the usual adult party wreckage, this time with what sounded like sirens, for some reason, but there was nobody around. The adults with kids had gone home. The others were on the back deck in the storm, re-enacting the sinking of the *Titanic*. Some were on their knees singing "Nearer My God to Thee," while others poured pitchers of ice cubes on their heads or gripped the railing, soaked and shouting, their dresses and glowing white shirts plastered against their chests by the force of the storm. Nick's parents were among the soaked and shouting.

But they must have been ready to leave. As soon as Josephine saw him she said something to Wolf, who came along without objection.

Whose sweater are you wearing? was the first thing Josephine said.

Worry about it in the morning, Wolf said, lifting his fedora from Nick's head.

As the three of them passed through the living room, Nick glimpsed, at the far end, stretched out alongside the piano, an encrusted orange man in dress pants and a white shirt open at the neck, with his head between facing speakers blasting the sounds of a four-alarm fire. It would turn out that the man's face, neck, hands, and bare feet were covered in Cheezies, individually attached by loops of Scotch tape. Thinking about it later, Nick realized that the idea must have been that the sirens, shouting firemen, and screams of people trapped in a burning building would jolt the man up thinking the house was on fire, and when his hand went to his face it would be Cheezie against Cheezie. But the man was as unrousable by the commotion of a house burning down around him as by the storm roaring through outside. He was peacefully at rest, at home in this.

You're an entity, Joe, Wolf observed as they passed through to the front hall.

Joe Kembley made no response.

‹ ‹ ‹

Outside, in the storm, Wolf wrapped Nick in his coat against the blast, which was so strong it would blow two of the Kembleys' iron patio chairs into the pool. As Wolf struggled with the rear door of the Dodge, Nick was looking up at the house and seeing, or thinking he was seeing, Bobby standing at his parents' bedroom window in his mother's top, watching them. Nick waved, but at that moment the wind folded the door back on its hinges so fast and hard that it smashed the side mirror, and in the shock of that, Nick couldn't be sure Bobby saw and waved back, or not.

That wasn't the usual dreaming ride home under his father's coat in the freezing back seat, but Nick clutching the back of the front seat with one hand and with the other holding the howling back door as shut as he could while watching through the slapping wipers the pavement in the headlights flowing like a river.

This is bad, Wolf said.

Let's just get home, Josephine said.

They were soaked and shivering.

Home was two minutes away. Before they got there, the street lights went out, and Nick wondered if sudden silence from the speakers on either side of Joe Kembley's head would wake him when the sounds of a four-alarm fire had failed to.

The headlights when Wolf pulled into their driveway illuminated a small yellow-brick house streaming with water. The barbecue lay overturned in the middle of the carport, which looked empty. Vacated.

Where's our trailer? Nick said, thinking the wind must have taken it.

The Cruisette? Wolf said. Why?

Over her shoulder Josephine said, I wondered when you'd finally notice. It's been gone a month. And then she said, Your father claimed it was time.

Why?

Ask your father.

It was time, Wolf said.

What about our holidays?

We've grown too big for it, Wolf said. We're going to have to figure out something else.

You're going to have to figure out something else, Josephine said.

It was normal for Nick's parents to round off a party with an argument. He would hear them downstairs, the cupboard doors opening and closing, the ice cube tray cracking, their voices conversational, and then the arguing. Later, shouting and slamming doors.

On the night of Hurricane Hazel there was no fight, only the roar of the storm. Perhaps they were abstracted, or cowed. Later everybody said it sounded like a freight train coming through. That was exactly what it sounded like. Later, closer to dawn, it sounded like nothing but wind and rain.

‹ ‹ ‹

By Sunday morning the sun was shining. Except for a foot of water in the basement — down from a peak of four feet early Saturday — and roads, sidewalks, and lawns strewn with branches and shingles and the river flats still under water, you would never know the weekend had started off with a hurricane. On Sunday afternoon Wolf got a call telling him that the flood had swept the Cruisette from its plug-in at the Valley Trailer Park and left it wedged in a partly submerged trailer jam at the foot of the bluff just west of the Kembleys'. After replacing the receiver, Wolf swung away from the phone and Nick was standing right there.

They'll fool ya, Wolf said bleakly.

So we've still got the Cruisette? Nick said.

Just, Wolf said, rubbing at his face. Barely. Maybe.

As soon as Wolf was out of earshot, Nick called Bobby and arranged to meet him at eight the next morning on the Kembley patio.

That night, sometime after one, too excited to sleep, Nick climbed out of his bedroom window and spread his bedding on the carport roof. At first light he climbed back inside for a kitchen chair, which he sat on out there, tilted back on its rear legs. In the Indian-summer, post-hurricane warmth of early morning, the street had a milky glamour. The septic, chalk odour of Humber River mud hung faint in the air. Now and then a car passed. Otherwise ecstatic ratchet-trill cicada choruses, impossible in October, soared and died, soared and died. The birdsong too grew more un-accountable the harder Nick listened.

His dog Elmer was with him, sitting with his weight pitched against Nick's leg, panting when he wasn't snapping at invisible flies. If Nick looked at him, Elmer would prick his ears and direct his attention to a point of interest perceptible only to himself. *Put aside all fear, for I am your dog*, Elmer's posture said. *Observe as I focus my superhuman vision and dogwhistle hearing upon this inconceivably remote threat to your well-being.* On Nick's first day home from hospital at the age of three days, Wolf whipped off his booties so Elmer could lick his feet. Let the dog get to know the new baby. This was Nick's first memory: the rasp of Elmer's tongue against the bottoms of his feet on his first day home. A lavish welcome. He looked at Elmer. When Elmer closed his greying muzzle and directed his attention to Nick's bedroom window, Nick looked too. They listened. It was the bathroom tap. It turned off. It turned on. Wolf was shaving. On a day when his shift at Kembley Cotton didn't start until four in the afternoon. This meant that if Nick tried to make it downstairs and out the door before Wolf finished shaving, Wolf would say from the mirror,

Nick, give me a minute here.

When Elmer's attention returned to the window, so did Nick's. Wolf's hands were lowering out a kitchen chair. When Nick looked again, Wolf was coming toward him with the chair. Like any person or dog, Wolf glanced away during the middle portion of his approach. But when Wolf did this, it was in the knowledge that unlike most people and all dogs he was coming at you with a destabilizing agenda. Sometimes in his father's presence Nick would feel a prickling sensation at the side of his face or the back of his neck. He'd whip around in time to see the baffled, brimming eyes veer away. When Wolf's eyes veered away during the middle portion of his approach, he wasn't regretting what he was about to do to your complacency, he was loving you with the complicated rage of a vandal hefting a hammer or a can of paint as he sizes up a statue or a blank wall.

Wolf placed his kitchen chair alongside Nick's then stepped to the edge of the carport roof and surveyed the street. When a car rocketed past, he said,

People are shocked when kids get hit by cars. The way people drive, they should be shocked more kids aren't hit by cars.

This was something Wolf did that Nick's mother called *reducing everything to zero*. He waited.

For you, Wolf continued as he stood looking down at the street, a day like this, a holiday you didn't see coming, will be a time pool, off to one side of the stream. Like a whirlpool, only calm. Memorable as long as you live. For me it's one more cup of coffee. A marker. A beat. They're all the same. One cup a day. Every time I turn around I'm pouring myself another cup. By the time you're my age, it feels like it's every hour. Of course, I've been working for the past twenty years. He looked around at Nick. How old are you now, thirteen?

Eleven.

Wolf returned his attention to the street.

When your grandfather was thirteen, Wolf said, he'd quit school and was working as a hooper's assistant in a barrel factory up Highway 32, past Gobel. I used to think we'd drive up there and I'd show you where your grandfather worked when he was your age, but last year the place burned down, for the insurance. Now all we'd see is a Dairy Queen. Nobody needs to drive thirty miles to see a Dairy Queen. What time is it?

Nick got out the watch. Half past.

Wolf looked at the watch. You don't have a watch, he said.

This is Mum's. She got that new one.

You don't want to be wearing your mother's watch.

I don't. I keep it in my pocket.

Half past what? Six?

Seven.

Jesus Christ. Wolf picked up his chair and crossed to the window. As Elmer and Nick watched, Wolf used the chair to climb back in, without lifting it in after him. They heard him go downstairs and fetch the paper from the front step and come back up to the bathroom and shut the door. Whereas most people spend the space of time before they move their bowels quietly alone, like animals, straightening knick-knacks, clipping their nails, eating grass if they could, Wolf spent it disconcerting people. If nobody was around, he disconcerted Elmer. Nick looked at the watch again to see the time but was so anxious that Wolf would prevent him from meeting Bobby to explore the Cruisette that it failed to register even as a timepiece. Wolf was easily capable of spending an hour on the toilet. He kept a stack of *Reader's Digest*s on the windowsill next to it, so that he could increase his word power while he stank up the second floor.

Eventually the toilet flushed, and Wolf lowered himself back out the window. Again he set the kitchen chair next to Nick's. But this time, placing one hand on Elmer's head, he remained standing, and the three of them spent a moment in silent contemplation of the chair.

Its backrest and seat were upholstered in tufted beige vinyl in a gold fleck, with nicked and lustreless gold piping, the vinyl split and slashed over time to reveal drifts of dirty stuffing. Both the backrest and the seat were bolted to a frame of squared, chromed tubing bubbled with corrosion. At their beat-up kitchen table, under the buzzing fluorescence, such a chair fit right in, it was perfect, a standard thing. On the carport roof in morning sunlight, it was a hogwhimpering eyesore.

We could use a new kitchen set, Wolf conceded as he took his seat in the chair, sliding down until the ridge at the rear of his skull hooked onto the top of the backrest. His head rotated, and he looked at Nick and said,

We won't be getting one soon.

Why? Did you quit the mills?

Wolf was always threatening to quit the mills.

That's what you'll tell people when they ask.

You *quit* the *mills*?

A conversation Joe Kembley and I were having at the party the other night entered a grey area, Wolf said. You know Joe inherited. He didn't work his way up through the shop. He's never really mastered the time and temperature protocols for Rhodamine No. 7 on unbleached, heavy-grade poplin. Sometimes you have to wonder how much he actually knows about the dye process. Anyway, one thing led to another. But let me be clear. Any Cheezie I touched I ate. These things are a lot of fun until somebody gets hurt.

You can always find another job, Nick said. This bland assurance left his mouth like shit from a shovel. It was something an adult would say, and then he remembered where and how often he'd heard it: from this man right here.

I've got holes bored, Wolf affirmed. If I could play people's games I'd be dangerous. But I know one thing. This is unlikely to have a positive effect on my relations with your mother.

Dad, what about the Cruisette?

The question seemed to catch Wolf unawares. As he considered his answer, he lifted one foot, straight out, and studied it. So did Nick.

It was a foot so broad and high-arched that the tongue of the shoe failed to span the vamp and so short and drake-broad from being so high-arched that the empty toe curled upward, like a pixie boot's. To Nick it had always been a wonder that with feet like that his father could walk at all, but the fact was, once Wolf hit his stride, he moved with impressive speed and grace.

Wolf lowered his foot. The Cruisette, he said, is something else again. He pushed himself off the chair and picked it up and stood looking down at Nick and said, What's happened to the Cruisette is what's happened to the Cruisette. It's not a sign. The only way it's a sign is of what can happen.

Saying this, Wolf carried the chair to the window, lifting it in after him.

With his father out of sight, Nick straightened his left leg and studied his own foot in its sneaker, angling it this way and that. To his surprise at one level and at another not, it was not his father's foot in the least. He saw his father, unlike himself, as a man leaning back in a frayed aluminum lawn chair at an unregulated intersection, arms upraised, big trucks blasting through, dust swirling all around. A man with little practical sense of danger, too interested in how things will go. A drunken conversation with his boss that loses him his job. The family Cruisette swept away in a flood and lodged in a trailer jam. These were the kinds of developments Wolf had no trouble getting with.

When Nick heard the front door, he stepped forward to the edge of the roof.

Hey Dad! Are you going to the Cruisette now?

Wolf was standing by the Dodge, patting his pockets for his keys. Not while it's still in the river, he said, half to himself. Shyly he touched the toe of his shoe to the rear door that had been blown back on its hinges. Not held entirely shut by rope, the door yielded a little to his foot. How do I feel about the Cruisette? Wolf asked, rhetorically. Numb, he answered, and was struck by a bolt of self-consciousness that half threw him into the car. He grabbed on to the frame and squinted up at Nick, seeming to wait.

Why? Nick said.

Wolf had disappeared. His reply was the engine starting. After a minute, he rolled down the window and stuck out his head. It's complicated, he said. And switched off the engine.

What? Nick said.

Loudly, from inside the car, Wolf said, Put Elmer on his chain. We're taking a walk.

‹ ‹ ‹

It wasn't easy boosting Elmer through the window and corralling him down to the backyard. Nick's unexpected holiday from school, along with Wolf's unprecedented appearance on the carport roof, had Elmer assuming that the normal course of the day had gone by the board. As Nick clipped his collar to the chain attached to the clothesline, Elmer shot aggrieved glances to the left and to the right. Passing back through the house, Nick checked his mother's watch. It was five past eight. He was already late meeting Bobby, who unless he went down to the river alone was now destined to fail to be among the first to explore the Cruisette after the flood. But what could Nick do? It was his father's will. When God told Abraham to kill Isaac, was Isaac asked how he felt about carrying the wood for the pyre? No. It would wreck the whole story.

At the bottom of their front walk, Nick turned north, but it was only him. He stopped and looked around. Wolf had stopped too and was looking back at him. Where are you going? Wolf said. So they weren't checking out the Cruisette after all. For Nick this was a familiar experience. Guilt-ridden pleasure in immunity from blame because his father didn't care or wanted him along or said it was okay, and then the disappointment.

The walk they took that morning was Nick's normal school-day walk but not today. Just keeping up with his father was exhausting. With his famished eyes and his terrible feet, his big hands on their long arms, the palms back-turned, Wolf moved in a hungry, loping prowl, at a tremendous rate of speed, homing in on his destination, eating the miles. Repeatedly Nick was forced to put on bursts of acceleration. They passed the lane to Kembley Cotton, where Wolf no longer had a job. They passed Our Lady of the Perpetual Help and the vicarage. They crossed the railroad tracks. They passed the Kingdom Hall and Karpils' Manifold Variety.

Before long they passed the school, now Sunday quiet. From here it was houses on both sides to the highway, which they crossed — there was no traffic; the Humber bridge was washed out — and walked down the middle of the gravel concession road that the street became south of the highway, until they reached a row of vehicles parallel-parked at a sandbag wall. After stepping through a gap in the wall, they paused a moment to study its zigzag course between the houses and away to the west, and Nick reflected how tempting it would be to pack your sandbags tight, to get the wall up as fast as you could, but pack them too tight and they would fail to fit snug enough against each other to keep the water out. There seemed to be a lesson in this, and he looked to his father for what it might be.

Wolf lifted his chin to indicate the sandbag wall. I don't believe in sandbagging, he said.

A gradual stinking slope of mud and flood garbage ended at the shore of what looked like a constantly-sliding-away brown lake in which stood, in facing rows, homes built on the town flood plain. The far shore looked so far away it could have been New York State. As they watched, a dead cow floated past, making slow revolutions. At one point it dipped then rose high a moment, as if for display. Farther downstream it glanced off one of the houses before continuing on. Against every upstream surface not piled with small debris, the current climbed back on itself in a standing wave. Each next house on either side of the street was deeper in. The farthest house, six or seven away, had water to the tops of its ground-floor windows and a mud line partway up the second storey.

For Nick, to experience the Humber in flood was to know that all it takes is more water than a riverbed can contain to turn a human habitation into a beleaguered shell, an out-of-place obstruction to the flow.

The sightseer standing next to Wolf was a stout man wearing a blue serge suit and unbuckled galoshes. Wolf placed a hand on his arm and said,

Nothing quite like a good flood.

From the look on his face, the man found this statement surprising. Roads had been washed out, houses swept off their foundations and smashed against bridges and retaining walls. People had died.

One of these a year, Wolf said, and this could be our Tigris and Euphrates rolled into one.

Now the man chuckled and shook his head as if delighted to be addressed from the ranks of the harmlessly insane. It was difficult for people with little experience of Nick's father to know when they were being casually tormented, whereas Wolf believed that people are capable of larger perspectives than you would conclude from their often-muted behaviour when they find themselves unexpectedly in the company of a wild thinker.

Twenty years ago, Wolf told the man, my father used to walk down here on Sundays with a sack over his shoulder and haul out eels with his bare hands.

When the man only speechlessly marvelled at this, making a clucking sound with his tongue, Wolf turned his attention to Nick. It was now Nick's arm he touched as he tipped his head toward the water and predicted, commanded, or advised,

You won't forget this.

It was a statement Nick heard as primarily intended for the man in the galoshes. Silently he vowed to expunge this entire experience from his mind for all time.

A reaction that has evidently had the opposite effect.

Behind them a flatbed truck pulled up. Four men in overalls leapt out and started removing sandbags from the wall and passing them into the back of the truck. Slowly Wolf looked around. Sandbaggers, he muttered scathingly.

Nick went over to where the men were working, but he could barely lift the one sandbag he tried. The sag of it made it unwieldy. He returned to his father.

They're heavy, Wolf said.

They should call them *sag*bags, Nick said. When Wolf didn't say anything, Nick said, I want to go home.

It wasn't home Nick wanted to go, it was to the Kembleys', to meet Bobby. To salvage their original intention. He was fishing in his pocket for his mother's watch when Wolf, without taking his eyes off the water, slipped off his own and passed it to him, saying,

We'll have the strap taken in.

Thank you very much, Nick said coldly. He didn't need two watches. He couldn't wear his mother's because it was a girl's and he couldn't wear his father's because the face of it would make his wrist look too small. He hated to think that the only reason his father was giving him his watch was that his mother had given him hers. And he hated to think that his father would make the presentation in the form of a casual hand-off to impress a stranger.

Just try not to lose it, Wolf said, but Nick was already walking away. As Nick passed beyond what was left of the sandbag wall, Wolf called out,

And don't go down to the Cruisette! I don't care how many kids are going!

Nick ignored this as also intended for the ears of a stranger. As he walked back up the street, he thought about cities buried under sand and villages inundated by dams, and he thought about digging or diving down and making discoveries that changed everything, and he thought of the water in his parents' basement Saturday morning, creeping up the steps, the walls, the furnace, clear and placid in the silence of the defeated sump pump. It was water-table water, not Humber water. It looked black, but when you cupped it in your hands it was so clear that it was all you could do not to drink it. Dive down with a light and there would be their old stuff in terrible underwater clarity.

In spring the Humber churned inside its banks like Quik in a Mixmaster. By August it was brown pools and shallow rapids amongst powdery white rocks. What Nick's father had taken him to see was a sliding-away lake of shit. What was submerged was not preserved and made visible, it was fouled and destroyed. His father had taken him to the flood to show him what the world does to human hopes and dreams. He wanted Nick to know that human beings are nothing before the force of the world. Any human hope or dream will soon be an empty impediment to the flood, and then it will be swept away.

‹ ‹ ‹

The Kembleys' big white house stood at the north end of a ten-acre lawn so lush it could have been Kentucky bluegrass.

When Nick was little he had once asked his father why they didn't have grass like that.

It's not available here, Wolf replied.

By the time Nick arrived at the Kembleys', it was nearly nine o'clock in the morning. When Dora Kembley answered the door, she placed her cigarette in her mouth and took Nick's hands in hers and said,

Joe feels terrible about what happened Friday night.

The Cruisette, I know, Nick said, extricating his hands.

In the dining room, Joe and Bobby were still at the breakfast table, looking unhappy. When they smiled they had the same smile, but unhappy they looked like two completely different people.

I've asked Wolf to reconsider, Joe told Nick.

I didn't even notice it was gone, Nick confessed.

The Cruisette? Joe said after a short pause. Anything of value lost there?

It was like Joe Kembley to adjust smoothly to Nick's concerns while remaining at least one step ahead. It hadn't occurred to Nick that the contents of the Cruisette could be lost, or destroyed. He'd imagined it floating, like a cork. He looked to Bobby, who mouthed, *Where were you?* Dora was gazing out the window at a black-capped chickadee swinging its beak from side to side, tossing seeds from the feeder, like a diner who'd had it with the fare. The seeds were clicking against the glass. Nick shrugged.

It's been a rough weekend for your dad, Joe said next. How's he doing?

Good, Nick said, and burst into tears.

This was unexpected, not least by Nick. Dora leaned across to hand him a napkin. It was a misunderstanding, Joe said.

When you fired him, Bobby said in a flat voice.

Door's open, Joe said. Door was never shut.

After Bobby was excused, the boys climbed the fence at the checkerboard sign at the top of the bluff and stood gazing down at the trailer jam. In all, they counted thirteen trailers in the jam proper and five others strewn along the riverbank like tossed shipping containers. Strangely, a motorboat was moored to the heap of trailers below them, drifting with the current.

As they started down the path Bobby said again, Where were you?

Nick told him.

Why didn't you come and get me?

How could I?

On your bike.

Sure, it sounds obvious when you say it.

Did you think your dad was taking you to check out the Cruisette?

Not really. Nick kept his burning face directed to where he was placing his feet.

As they came down the hill through the trees, they could tell the high-water mark from where the mud started. They took off their sneakers and socks and proceeded in bare feet. Soon the mud line was climbing the tree trunks. On the valley floor they could almost touch the highest clumps of drying grass and shredded garbage caught on bushes and branches. Straight ahead, across the silted, hummocky, stinking flats, they could see a trailer wrapped around a willow. They left their sneakers on a rock and waded through the muck in the direction of the trailer jam, which was farther upstream, against the bluff, on the narrow margin between it and the brown torrent.

The water was receding fast. Already the motorboat they had seen from the top of the bluff sat angled in the mud.

After some searching, they found the Cruisette wedged in a particularly compacted section of the jam, close to the foot of the bluff. Reaching it meant squeezing between a crushed Overlander and another ruptured mass of aluminum and soggy particleboard. As they approached, a pink rubber boot nudged the door open, and a shovel ejected a dump of mud. And then a pretty woman in a T-shirt, shorts, and pink rubber boots leaned out and was looking at Nick.

I know who you are, she said.

What are you doing in our Cruisette? he asked her.

Oh, just mucking about. Could you tell him the water's down enough now?

Did you lose your own trailer? Bobby asked the woman.

This question she rewarded with a beautiful smile. No, I don't have a trailer, she said. But thank you for asking.

Can we see inside? Nick said.

The woman made a show of flattening herself against one side of the doorway, and they looked in. It stank. They saw a bed, a cookstove, a fold-down table with two chairs upturned on it. Everything was thickly and smoothly coated in mud, except for the floor, which the woman had been scraping at with the shovel.

‹ ‹ ‹

As Nick and Bobby squeezed back down the passageway between the Overlander and the other wreck, Nick said,

She seems nice.

How does she know your dad?

Whose dad? Wolf said, stepping around the end of the Outlander. His pants were rolled to his knees, and his shoes were in his hand. His eyes shifted to the Cruisette, where he must have seen the woman standing in the doorway, because next he called out,

I'm on my way!

Nick started to turn to see if he could see her around the bulge in the Overlander, but an unnatural, pleading quality in his father's voice as he called out caused Nick to swing back, and he was sorry he did, because Wolf was looking at him again, now with a smile that Nick wouldn't see again until eighteen years later, in a news box on the street: Martin

Hartwell's, as he waved from his stretcher while being carried from the plane crash he'd survived by eating one of the dead, a nurse. It was the smile of a man happy to be back, but it was also the smile of a man who knows that nobody comes back from this.

How bad is it? Wolf asked.

Fairly bad, Nick said.

‹ ‹ ‹

As Nick and Bobby retraced their steps through the mud, Nick regretted including his friend in this adventure, and he worried that when they reached the rock where they'd left their sneakers Bobby would want to sit down and talk about what had just happened at the Cruisette. Bobby had a corny need sometimes to get to the bottom of things, whereas Nick preferred a more oblique approach.

When they reached the rock, Nick said he needed to get going.

Bobby just looked at him.

What? Nick said.

They were climbing the hill before Bobby said, So you never saw her before?

No, why should I of?

Your dad knows her.

I doubt it.

He knew she'd be there.

Yeah, right.

At the top of the hill, Bobby said, My dad didn't really mean to fire your dad.

I know. He quit.

Will you tell him my dad wants him back?

Why should I? What if he doesn't feel like working for a jerk?

Bobby sighed and turned away. Okay, see you then! he called over his shoulder in the odd, polite way he sometimes had, as Nick headed down the blue Kembley lawn toward home.

His mother was in the front yard, mowing a different order of lawn, with crabgrass and dead patches. When she saw Nick, she looked at his legs, and then she turned off the mower.

You went down to the river.

When Nick looked where his mother was looking, he saw a band of beige above his socks. When he looked back at her she wasn't angry, but she seemed tired.

Where's your father?

Nick shook his head. And then he said, At work? When she didn't say anything, he added, I guess I'll take a shower.

That's what I could use every hour of my life, she said, and gave a yank on the cord.

Nick was out the back door before the lawn mower finally started. Elmer was overjoyed to see him. He wagged wildly, his dewlaps lifting with such energy that successive fits of sneezing nearly dashed his head against the ground. Nick fell to his knees to unclip Elmer's chain from his collar while Elmer rubbed his muzzle against Nick's chest and burrowed it in under his arm with the ardent pressure of canine devotion.

MISS BUFFETT

The dreams of the vicar-general have hit the wall. They have backed up and tried again. Damaged now, no traction, memory leaking. Futility. He's awake. The birds are already at it, sparrows in the oak. The next time he comes round it's the *too-wheedle* of a jay, revolving in his head like a blue crank. But when he knows that implicated in everything, all night, like a refrain or a kind of problem, it's been Miss Buffett, gone but not gone, never gone, he can only pretend he's not awake.

He extricates his feet from the tangle of sheets and swings his legs to the floor. Rubs his shanks.

Down the hall he feels under the desk for the *On* button. The computer fan starts up like a vacuum cleaner. This will take a few minutes. He showers. By the time he has dried himself the computer is booted. The last time he looked, which was last night, he had an hour free after lunch. Now a delegation of Japanese schoolchildren will see him on their way to Banff. By the dark art of Appointment Reminder, Father Brigilio has written them in from his office down the hall.

When the knock comes, the vicar-general is wandering through his chambers, part praying, part meditating, part expecting this to be Miss Buffett. Last night, while she was chorusing in his head, a group from the residence was downtown seeing a revival of *Oklahoma!* Brigilio enters with a jazz pirouette double turn. As he helps the vicar-general finish dressing, they could be in a musical, and all the way down the hall to the elevator, as he tells him about the show, he does little winding steps. This is a man who has seen productions of *Oklahoma!* in New York, Chicago, Toronto, Minneapolis, and Hartford, Connecticut. The vicar-general is amazed how much one individual can know about one old musical.

In the refectory, they join the others, who are also still excited from the show.

When the vicar-general murmurs, Sorry now I missed it, Father Brigilio looks at him and then he looks away.

Eventually the priests stop vying for the vicar-general's attention. His forbearance is his authority, and by their postures and readiness to laugh and the higher pitch of their voices he is made aware of his power. They share with him their pleasure in the show and they give him their deference. What can he say? He wasn't there. Please, he'd said when Father Brigilio pleaded with him to come too. Even just to get out and relax for a change. But when the day came, what a relief it was to watch them all pile into the Suburban and drive away. He tried to read but kept dozing off and so went to bed, but it was too early, and he couldn't sleep, and so he took a pill, and when he did sleep, the fabric of his dreams was Miss Buffett, and here we are.

The talk has turned to Father Hickey, who is dying, and to the cardinal's dinner, at the golf club tonight.

⟨ ⟨ ⟨

After breakfast, in the elevator, the vicar-general says to Father Brigilio, They're good men. If they didn't have to be priests they'd be heroes.

Now, Billy.

The outside air is warm, the sky is grey. Oh what a beautiful morning! Brigilio observes in a light baritone.

You want to see it again.

Don't get your hopes up. But if I shift the vestry meeting on the twenty-third, we could make the Wednesday matinee — assuming I can get tickets.

You'll get tickets.

Chicks and ducks and geese better scurry.

Last night when they got back, Brigilio parked the Suburban at the far edge of the lot, under the willows. Now yellow-green pollen hangs off it in folds, like drapery. He helps the vicar-general in. As he comes around to the driver's side he does a *relevé*, and then with his finger he writes on the hood, *Lava me*.

⟨ ⟨ ⟨

Their destination is a cathedral beyond the western limit of Aspen Estates. Our Lady of Assisi has been paid for by Ed-Gas, through the Ron and Barb Jackman Foundation. The project was a long time in development, but once completed it made a perfect capstone to the career of the vicar-general's predecessor, who, to this end, had cultivated a strong working relationship with Ron Jackman. The vicar-general's relationship with Ron Jackman has not been so strong. He understands fundraising, as he must, and has done his share, but he's tired now, and he's tired of being used and seeing the Church used, and the Jackmans are the kind of Catholic who give big when it suits them, but you don't see them in church unless a family member has died or they want a church wedding.

You see them, that is, if you perform the service, which in the case of the Jackmans the vicar-general has done twice now, telling himself he had a choice. You want to be rigorous, but you don't want to become flinty. Neither do you want to turn into a salesman in a collar, but you're not a fool, and so you do it. You tell yourself that by the light of your mercy a Jackman may yet be truly drawn into the fold. And then one Sunday you're visiting a church in another diocese, sitting behind the pulpit, next to the choir, sideways to the congregation, while the priest says the homily. You're here to offer Mass, and you're waiting to do that, just sitting there, bored, weary, depressed, thinking about this and that, rubbing your temples, checking your nails, fiddling with your ring, when you look up, straight into the eyes of the altar boy who's been watching you from his seat at the far side of the altar. If the look in the kid's eyes was contempt or even disdain, that would be one thing, but it's disappointment, and there is little you can disagree with in that. And you think, *My son, this is nothing.*

Twice now for the Jackmans the vicar-general has agreed to do a service. And their insouciance in the face of this dispensation struck him as strange until it came to him, oh right, they've given twenty-six million. And he found himself, on the first occasion, gazing into a coffin at a waxen face he had never seen before in his life, and on the second, at an insecure, overweight young woman standing beside a slippery-eyed character in a goatee, smelling of liquor, and he felt like an executioner. At the wedding reception, which by not attending he would have undone any conceivable good that might have come of his presiding at the service in the first place, most people from their questions had no idea what a vicar-general was. So are you above a bishop or not? one woman interrupted impatiently when he started to explain. And nobody knew how to talk to him any more than he knew how to talk to them. They couldn't wait for him to leave so they could have a little fun.

And so, when the spa being built on the roof of the Jackmans' 40,000-square-foot home was nearly finished and Ron Jackman called him up to let him know he should feel free to swing by any time to bless it, just give him a week-or-two warning, he wanted to have some people over, the vicar-general said he couldn't do it.

What? You want to just drop in? Hey! I need notice! We'll have a do!

No. Bless your spa.

The vicar-general didn't hesitate to refuse Jackman, but the call ended too abruptly and the receiver came down too hard for the reaction to be disappointment or belated embarrassment at the egregiousness of the request. Six weeks later the man was back, this time in person, with a different request, or test: a ceremony of Special Blessing for Our Lady of Assisi. Although the same age as the vicar-general, Jackman could pass for two decades younger. The vicar-general has been mistaken for eighty, Jackman's had work done, as Father Brigilio noticed the first time he picked him out across a room. Having already refused the man once, the vicar-general began their conversation about a Special Blessing by assuring him he'd be happy to raise with the Events Council any suggestions he might have as to —

Okay, first things first. Who's doing it?

That would depend. Tell me what you have in mind. We've already had the Dedication —

Yeah, but that's standard. I'm talking about a special occasion. What would you say to the Holy Father?

What would I *say* to him?

Okay. Look. This is easily the finest cathedral — and Jackman took a newspaper clipping from his pocket and waved it in the air. He didn't need to read it out to the vicar-general, who knew which one it would be, a civic pride piece in the *Journal*. I say we go for it. We get the Holy Father in to do a Special Blessing.

Still the vicar-general didn't understand. And then he did and was dumbfounded.

When he's back in Canada, Jackman said.

But that's not for two years —

Time to make our case.

And only Toronto and Montreal —

So they adjust his plans. Come *on*, man! Two years!

Mr. Jackman, the Vatican isn't going to change the Holy Father's itinerary just so —

Thanks for the advice, your Grace, Jackman said, already on his feet, turning to leave.

‹ ‹ ‹

Our Lady of Assisi stands pinked by the rising sun against the grey sky. Towering over the wheat fields on its west side and the new homes crowding its east flank, it's no less solitary and strange than a mosque in a forest clearing or a Hindu temple hard against a gas refinery or a driving range.

The vicar-general and Father Brigilio are here to say the 7:45 a.m. weekday Mass. The acre parking lot is empty.

Lotsa stucco, Father Brigilio says, and the vicar-general thinks what he thinks every morning: this should still be farmland.

There will be no altar boy, no choir. In the sacristy Father Brigilio helps the vicar-general on with his alb and cassock. Fetches him his zucchetto. He then stands in the doorway, reporting. The Faithful Five, now down to Four, he says. Absent the departed. Really strange to see her not out there.

And for the vicar-general, last night's dream is back, a symphony of indignation, broadcasting through her. The dreamer, who has caught only the gist, thinks, It's a good thing Miss Buffett's communications come with simultaneous translation in slough algae. But it seems not all sloughs are translation-grade, and the ones that are can be hard to access. Searches go out, but sinkholes yawn and erratics loom. Back up and try again.

You know, weekdays we should be using the south transept, Brigilio says as he turns from the doorway. Cozier.

Talk to the Liturgy Committee.

Naw, let's just do it. No Miss Buffett to rat us out, bless her. Maybe I'll get the car washed, while you're — Brigilio's frowning at his BlackBerry.

The cathedral smells of fresh-cut travertine. When the plans call for this much stained glass, you hire an artist, not an interior decorator. The morning sun illuminates an ecclesiastical space of magnificent banality. There is the emptiness, and then there is the plaster-saint, church-art box it comes in. The congregation is four women and a child in a bassinet. Two of the women are Italian, a mother and her daughter, or perhaps sister. Across the aisle, the other two women, and presumably the infant, are Chilean. Sisters, the vicar-general has assumed. They have all come out here on the first No. 6 bus of the day. The vicar-general makes the sign of the cross. He begins the Greeting.

Afterward the congregation slips out with the discretion of indentured servants. The infant hasn't made a sound. Back in the sacristy, Father Brigilio pops shut the holster of his Black-Berry. It's taken him twenty-five minutes to get through to the box office, but he's got the tickets and is singing, *Ooooklahoma, where the wind comes sweepin' down the plain — !*

‹ ‹ ‹

At the car wash, the manager, a large man with an earring, leans across to finger a chip in the windshield. He looks at them sorrowfully through the glass. He crouches at Brigilio's window. These things radiate, he says.

Basic inside and out, Brigilio says.

The manager does his clipboard scrawl. Crouches again. Any windshield washer fluid in the rear of the vehicle, gentlemen, I suggest you take it in with you. Folks in there drink the stuff.

He moves away.

Prick, Brigilio says.

As Brigilio pays at the cash, the vicar-general stands at the first window and watches the suds hammer down on a black BMW 7 Series sedan, moving slowly forward on the belt.

Brigilio comes over and stands beside him and watches too. The next vehicle is a rusted-out Mazda pickup. As one they step to the next window. Here a Native woman in a Clash T-shirt stands waiting for the BMW, a rag in her hand. A few feet from her, also waiting, also holding a rag, is an Ethiopian-beautiful black kid, no more than fourteen or fifteen. The kid glances at them without interest. The Native woman does not look at them at all. Right now for her this is not a window. Against the far wall stands an industrial washing machine. The third worker, a bum in baggy jeans and a flannel shirt in faded blue plaid, is removing armfuls of rags, piling them on the metal table alongside. As the other two set to work wiping down the BMW, the bum continues at the table, his back turned, folding rags. And then he picks one up and swings toward the car. His lower face is hidden under a prophet's beard, but there is something familiar about the eyes.

McGuigan, Brigilio says.

So it is. In the early days of Vatican II, in the sixties, the days of the Plunge, Brian McGuigan was their City of

Champions Plunger Extraordinaire. They'd hang around Boyle Street without a collar, penniless, no place to lay their heads. Seeing the world through homeless eyes, like rolling stones, was the idea. When John XXIII put an end to such foolishness, McGuigan kept his head down, and twenty years later he and the vicar-general were ordained at the same Mass, and McGuigan became a bishop in Saskatchewan, where, inside a year, his diocese ran into stewardship problems. According to some reports he was secretly funnelling Church funds to radical Church movements in South America, according to others he was secretly funnelling Church funds to unauthorized assistance for the homeless of Saskatoon, Regina, Medicine Hat. When the archbishop called him in, McGuigan minimized, temporized, apologized. When that didn't work, he denied everything, and when the archbishop slid the audit across the desk toward him, McGuigan fell to his knees and begged forgiveness. No dice. Fool with the kids, they move you. Fool with the money, you're out.

He's seen us, Brigilio says, ventriloquist-style.

McGuigan is beaming his big smile at them. Is he drunk? With a rag draped over an arm, he cocks a leg and indicates his attire with a what-can-I-say shrug. The Native woman glances over at him, and though there is no visible trace of impatience or censure on her face, McGuigan immediately leans hard with the rag into the far side of the BMW.

The vicar-general and Father Brigilio return to the first window in time to watch the Suburban come through. The Ethiopian kid is inside it with a cloth. They follow its progress as they followed the BMW's. When it reaches McGuigan, he betrays no sign he's aware they're watching again, but of course he knows a Church Suburban. And then it's ready to go, and he's the one who drives it out to the pickup area. My pleasure, your Graces, he says, extracting the necessary receipt from among the various flyers and slips of paper Brigilio holds out to him.

How are you, Brian? the vicar-general says.

Not too bad, Your Grace. Up and down. McGuigan is searching the vicar-general's face. You?

The vicar-general smiles. I'm fine, he says. A little tired.

Still working you too hard, are they?

Works himself too hard, Brigilio says.

Leopards and their spots, isn't it, McGuigan says, and glances at the Native woman. All right, take care of yourself, okay, Your Grace? You too, Father.

As they pull away, Brigilio says, I always liked the guy.

The vicar-general doesn't respond. He's thinking about Miss Buffett out in Clareview, living in the attic of her cousin's garage.

When he climbs the dry-rotted stairs to the landing and knocks, there is no answer. With his foot he nudges aside a rock painted to look like a sleeping rabbit and opens the door on darkness. His eyes adjust to a malachite jewel box of a room. An incensed grotto.

He repositions the rock and descends the stairs.

Nobody home, he says.

You think so? Brigilio says. You don't think he's where he always wanted to be? With the down-and-out, in the real world?

The vicar-general looks at Brigilio. He doesn't know what he's being asked.

No, eh? Brigilio says.

‹ ‹ ‹

At the seminary, the Japanese students have already arrived, and after they leave, Father Brigilio drops the vicar-general at the Misericordia before continuing on to do errands. He'll pick him up at three. Father Hickey's cancer has metastasized. He's in a double room on the eighth floor. In the other bed is Gordon, who is ninety-six and lies with his arms crossed over his chest, like an effigy. Father Hickey involves Gordon in the vicar-general's visit without placing any expectation on Gordon that he will respond, which Gordon does not.

In the vicar-general's first year at the seminary in Winnipeg, Father Hickey was the teacher who shuffled the halls in mink slippers. If you found yourself getting on the elevator with him, before you knew it the doors had closed and he was into a story about his mother making him wear short pants when he was fifteen, and before you had your balance he'd slip in something outrageous that made you laugh at the same time as it shocked you a little, keeping you at a distance, and when the doors opened he'd express a regret that you and he had to part but satisfaction too that you would continue this another time, because didn't you have the rest of your lives? And so they did. And in the eighties, when Rome was tossing wet blankets on social action, Father Hickey went back to the night parks and public toilets, or maybe he just grew more reckless, and it was the vicar-general who faced down the commissioner on the indecency charge. It was also the vicar-general who later signed the papers that made Father Hickey, at age seventy-eight, resident pastor of the

Seven Sorrows halfway house, on Boyle Street. It was the vicar-general to whom Father Hickey said softly, I want you to know, Bill, I don't hold you responsible for this.

Now Father Hickey is looking at him. You look beat, he says. When the vicar-general just shakes his head, he says, Listen. She drove you crazy. She drove us all crazy. You loved her. We all did. You're in mourning.

I'm a shell.

Tell me about it. When I got the diagnosis, I thought, I can handle this. I know about suffering. Christ wrote the book. Well, I was closer to Him in the parks. I'm thinking, Please God, don't tell me my spiritual life has been an accident of good health, and when health goes, the spirit goes, because at this rate I'll die an animal, beyond prayer. So last rites then a pillow over the face. I'll be fine with it. And Gordon won't tell a soul. Will you, Gord?

Father Hickey's eyes close. After a few minutes he says, A priest is a boy and then he's an old man.

‹ ‹ ‹

The vicar-general leans heavily on the arm of Father Brigilio as they make their way from the Suburban to the seminary door. His body knows that if it doesn't conserve its energy now, it'll need to dig too deep to get through the cardinal's dinner tonight. He has an hour. Immediately he falls asleep. When the knock comes, it's Father Brigilio, who leans in to say,

Why don't we just not go? I'll say you're indisposed. We don't have to stay.

They've added a private reception before the dinner, at the Jackmans'. When the vicar-general's eyes close at this, Brigilio adds, So we didn't get the second invitation in time.

It's on their roof?

How did you know?

‹ ‹ ‹

The reception is reached by a glass elevator that offers a view of the ginkgo tree and the two-storey living wall in the main foyer. The vicar-general and Father Brigilio step out amidst black ties and ball gowns. The rooftop is bordered on three sides by a copper railing, which overlooks the sixteenth hole of the Primrose Golf and Country Club. On the fourth side, reflecting the glittering company, is a fifteen-foot gold mirror. The air is soft and clear. The sun won't be down until nine. Cardinal Seward greets them warmly. Hold this, he says to Father Brigilio, handing him a champagne glass. A basset-eyed man five-six in elevator heels, the cardinal clasps the vicar-general's right hand in both his, against his heart, touching his forehead to the vicar-general's shoulder. How's it goin', Billy?

Not too bad, Your Eminence.

Hey, Brigilio, the cardinal says, stepping back and retrieving his glass. Always good to see you too. You fellows look like you need a drink. The cardinal beckons to a waiter, and then he says,

So, Brigilio, what's your handicap?

My reflux acts up at these things.

The cardinal laughs. *Golf*, man!

It also acts up when I play golf.

The cardinal talks about Father Frechette's latest, an allusion in a print interview in Red Deer last week to the sorry history of Ukrainian anti-Semitism, which has gone viral. Ukrainian Catholics across the country are up in arms.

Maybe a clarification, the vicar-general suggests.

I don't think so, the cardinal says. Sure, Danny misspoke, but that's Danny. These wing nuts'll tell you to your face the pogroms are Jewish lies. A statement from me and there's no end to it. Has anybody read a story lately about a Native who had one positive experience at a residential school?

Ron Jackman's standing just outside their circle, checking his phone. When the cardinal notices him he steps back, making room. Ron, you know these guys. To Father Brigilio and the vicar-general, the cardinal says, You know, Ron here's the next best thing to a priest: a Catholic and a golfer.

Jackman looks pleased. I wish I was, more than once a month. I figured if I lived close enough, but — Here he does a helpless shrug, and the cardinal laughs.

It's just holes in the ground, my friend, the cardinal says, scanning the crowd. You know all about them.

Now the vicar-general is presented with a tray containing a dozen glasses of red wine. He takes one, the tray moves on, and directly in front of him is Barb Jackman, telling him about Shar in China on her way to India in a convoy of Mercedes with a Rinpoche who cures people by blowing on them. The vicar-general doesn't know who Shar is. Let's see your wrist, Barb says, and before he has processed this she grabs his hand and lifts the wrist to her mouth and blows on it, a hot little gust. Pushing his hand back down to his side, she says,

You won't believe this, but you know what Shar's latest thing is? Buddhist nun. She wants to be a Buddhist nun! Isn't that a riot? Who even knew they *had* them?

Shar, he realizes, must be Charmaine, the daughter. And then he thinks, *But I just married her, to the shifty guy.*

Barb has read his face. She laughs. Actually, that didn't work out. I guess you didn't know Barry was Jewish. Not practising, but Hebrew school, bar-mitvahed, the whole shtick. But you know kids. You try telling them, but their love is bigger than cultural differences blah blah, and I'm like, *Hello?* and the next thing you know it's — and here she croons *I've grown disgusted with your race* and claps a hand over her mouth and looks around, mouthing *Aren't I awful?*

The reception is being held on the Jackmans' roof because on the other side of that fifteen-foot gold mirror is their new spa. Now the wall, which is cunningly in panels, retracts, to applause.

That's more like it, the cardinal says into the hush that falls. Let's have a look at these amenities.

Everybody presses forward. They want a look too. The vicar-general hears a woman explaining to her friend that the reason Ron and the cardinal are out of sight right now is Ron will be showing him the changing room off the new master bedroom, and next to it the Turkish bath.

After Jackman and the cardinal return to view, walking through the part of the spa now visible — weight machines, a massage table, a whirlpool tub — Ron drawing his attention to what looks from here like gold-plated faucets, the cardinal addresses the crowd concerning the delightfulness of the occasion, the generosity of the Jackmans, and how easy it would be for a broken-down old churchman to grow accustomed to such comforts. Before the laughter dies, he turns — and what could be more natural? — to bless the facilities, in English and Latin, sprinkling holy water from a vial he has taken from his pocket. It's all over in three minutes, and did that hurt? The Jackmans are beaming, the cardinal can do this kind of thing in his sleep, and everybody's pleased to have been included on a guest list that has them on this wonderful rooftop deck on one of those timeless prairie summer evenings when you can't believe that last February you were ready to slit your wrists if Ed didn't get that transfer to Vancouver. The vicar-general looks to Father Brigilio, and he doesn't know what he's thinking, not really, but he knows it's not about where they live or don't live, and then he looks over at Archbishop Ludoviccio, who has a hand on the shoulder of his yellow-haired priest and is saying something in his ear.

But now that the spa has been blessed, the reception is over. People are waiting for the elevator or starting down the marble staircase. The women will need time to freshen up.

The vicar-general and Father Brigilio walk together to the clubhouse.

‹ ‹ ‹

The Kashe Room in the Primrose Golf and Country Club is filled with the setting sun. The vicar-general and Father Brigilio have been seated at a table to the left of the head table, which is reserved for the archbishop, his priest, the cardinal, the Jackmans, and another big-donor couple.

The vicar-general and Father Brigilio sit facing each other across their table, in the company of three couples. On the vicar-general's right is Dolly Sproule, whose husband Fred owns the Kashe Drug chain. On his left is Big Al Loshak of Loshak Construction. Dolly and the Loshaks are church-goers, though not so much Al as his wife Eunice, who sits at Al's left. The other couple, Trish and Gerry Vernon, on either side of Father Brigilio, have just moved up from Calgary, where Trish was a going concern at St. Mary's. The vicar-general is meeting the Vernons for the first time. Brigilio knew them in Calgary, when he worked for the bishop. Gerry's in nanotechnology, with a government con-tract through the university.

If these dinners are work, people like this should make it easy, but the vicar-general hasn't been doing so well lately with people in large groups. On the Jackmans' roof, on his first wind, with Brigilio and the cardinal and Jackman all aw-shucks in the cardinal's company, and the chatter and the brays of laughter on every side dissipating into the eve-ning sky, he could manage. Here in this hot room with the setting sun lighting up the dust-coated floor-to-ceiling win-dows and the din of talk, it's all he can do not to put his head down on the table and weep.

Your Grace, Dolly Sproule says after the food has come, you're hardly touching your grub. I've been watching you.

Not much appetite tonight, Dolly —

I know. Another Rubber Chicken Special, right? Can I ask you something? Is it my imagination, or have you been a bit down lately?

More tired I would say, Dolly.

Well, what is that about?

Oh, you know. Stresses and strains. Not getting younger —
When *ever* are they going to let you people marry?
Startled, he looks at her. Smiles.

And I just want you to know, she adds, I include same-sex in that.

Good old Dolly, he thinks. What he says is, That would be a different Church.

Well, maybe it's time it was a different Church. She looks at him defiantly as she says this, he can feel God's love for her, and then she changes the subject.

The servers are still passing out the tiramasu when the speeches start, but there are only three. The cardinal knows how to hold a fundraiser. The speeches from Bishop Regan, head money hunter for the archdiocese, and Lester Jones, director of the Catholic Social Network, come in under ten minutes. The third speaker is the cardinal himself, who begins with a confession: he's sitting on fantastic news. He then speaks anecdotally for twenty minutes about the joys of charitable giving before telling his audience that they heard it here first: As everybody knows, in two years' time the Holy Father will be returning to Canada. What they don't know, but what they'll read in the weekend papers, is that on his way from Montreal to Vancouver he'll be paying a four-hour visit to this very city, where he'll conduct a Special Blessing of Our Lady of Assisi.

This certainly is fantastic news. People look at each other in wonder before rising to their feet to give the cardinal a standing ovation. Big Al Loshak, who with Fred Sproule remains seated, leans across to Fred and rasps, louder because of the applause than he intends,

Musta set Ronnie back half as much again as the goddamn land and construction put together.

‹ ‹ ‹

The Cemetery of the Holy Martyr was once a gay cruising
paradise heavy in springtime with the Tree-of-Heaven fra-
grance of balsam poplar. Now big houses with three-car
garages crowd in. As Father Brigilio steers the Suburban
through the gates, the vicar-general remembers Father
Hickey's groan of laughter when he learned that his choice
of resting place had been engulfed by a West Edmonton
housing development.

Just be gentle, he said, wiping his eyes. I bruise easily.

Something else that would have amused Father Hickey
was the late, surprise arrival at his funeral earlier in the
day of Archbishop Ludoviccio. Less surprising to Father
Hickey would have been the presence of Miss Buffett, like
a revenant in a dream, who had to be bodily removed from
the church. *And as they enter the gates she is already at
the graveside, patiently waiting to create her second distur-
bance of the day.*

How did she get here so fast?

Who get here? Brigilio says.

The archbishop's car is pulling in alongside them. His
dirty-white poodle with its coiffed face stares at them from
the back seat.

What the heck's Ludo's game? Brigilio says.

When Ludoviccio's gorilla face looms at his window, Brigilio pretends to give a start. The archbishop is not amused.
Who were those people? he says through the glass. Brigilio

lowers it and presses himself back in his seat. The vicar-general leans across him and waits. The archbishop wants to know why half the mourners at the service were street people.

They loved him, the vicar-general says.

Wrong answer. The archbishop rotates his body — as he needs to, his spine is fused — and says to his priest, Jim, call the police.

And then the archbishop's face is gone, and the yellow-haired priest is standing with one elbow on the roof of the archbishop's car with a cellphone at his ear.

Speed-dial, Brigilio mouths.

The clerics leave the archbishop's poodle barking into the gap of a lowered window, its teeth flashing yellow in its red mouth. They proceed two by two to the top of the parking lot. When they reach the hearse, which has pulled alongside the lower edge of the lawn, they wait without speaking as the funeral home men unload the casket onto a cart. The archbishop leans hard on his cane, breathing heavily. And then he and the vicar-general move forward, and the funeral home men push and pull the rack behind them down the grassy aisle. *At the end of it Miss Buffett stands waiting, her hands clasped over the enormous pink bow at her pudendum.*

In the distance, the crunch of tires on gravel. Send in the clowns. Half the mourners are Father Hickey's former divinity students and half are from the congregations of the two parishes he served for forty-six years. The street people whose attendance at the funeral has offended the archbishop have failed to show. Probably they couldn't afford the bus fare. Or the transfer at 178 Street has thrown them.

Miss Buffett's eyes close as she sways to the right, open as she sways to the left. Open they fix on the archbishop. Her lips are barely moving, but her neck muscles are working. Issuing from her are a thousand muffled voices. Miss Buffett was never a street person, she preferred the Central Library, where they'd catch her spitting in books she deemed anti-papist. More often, she'd take off her belt and use the notches to measure *Catholic Digest* font sizes. On Thursday afternoons, when she played checkers with Father Hickey in the basement of Seven Sorrows, the vicar-general imagined a bunker floor to ceiling with Flash Gordon crystal sets picking up frequencies dedicated to every query, cry, assertion, moan, bark, and whisper of the suffering city. Sometimes, depending on the course of the game, these would merge and swell into arias, duets, choruses, choirs. As the funeral home men position the coffin on the grave-mouth straps, two RCMP officers take up positions among the mourners directly behind her, but they don't see her. They're looking around as if to understand why they're here.

The vicar-general says the Blessing. When he finishes, the archbishop clears his throat. He arrived at Father Hickey's funeral too late to speak. Now he studies the faces of the mourners because he intends to do so now, and the vicar-general thinks,

Ludo, you've never set foot in Seven Sorrows. You never knew the man. You have never laid eyes on the old queen. You have no idea what his ministry has meant to people. You have no right to speak to his memory.

But the archbishop does speak, and he has three things to say. The first is that political action is a temporal expedient and cannot deliver us from our condition; only Christ can do that. The second is that the responsibility of the clergy is to minister to all people, not just to the poor. The third is that if you look hard enough, of course you will find filth in the Church, because there is filth in all humanity, by no means least in the media that it should be engaged in a systematic campaign to magnify the human frailty of priests.

As the vicar-general listens, he is aware that Father Brigilio, who is on his left, would like his attention. But the archbishop is scanning for disaffection in the ranks, and the vicar-general keeps his gaze on the big windows of the nearest monster home, not fifty metres away, blank reflectors with pencil lattices. And then the archbishop has finished speaking. The faces of the clergy remain carefully composed. The other mourners appear simply unfazed, as if this is the sort of thing an archbishop can be expected to say at a gravesite. The coffin is creaking downward.

And then Brigilio places a hand on his arm, and the vicar-general does look, and, well, if it isn't. A ragged mob is limping through the gates. They must have got lost or missed the transfer, or this is simply how long it takes to get out here by bus. When the vicar-general asked the delegation of Japanese high school students who came to see him this morning what city they were from, a girl perhaps fifteen gave him a quizzical look and said,

Hiroshima? You know? and making an expanding-outward gesture with her hands, like a flower opening, she asked shyly, Boom?

When you enter the seminary at seventeen or eighteen, you're still a child. You're there because a priest you respect has counselled you to tear up your university acceptance and break the chains of family and follow your vocation, and the door has clicked shut behind you, and nothing must pass beyond these walls. Not the nicknames, not the fist fights, not the sex, not the fervour, not the mortifications. You're not even allowed down to the foyer when your mother brings you clean laundry. The laundry of the boys without parents or with parents in other parts of the country, or the world, was done by Father Hickey, who assured them it took no more effort than only doing his own. With the casual selfishness of youth, the boys found this easy to believe.

The motley crowd has arrived. Deferential, it stands coughing and fidgeting several steps behind the other mourners.

The cranking stops. The coffin is as deep as it will go. *Miss Buffett's eyes are rolling in her head.* She was a tiny woman-child who looked fifty but could have been sixty. Most days she was kitted out the way she is today, like a madhouse Connie Stevens, in scuffed lace-up white go-go boots; nylons torn at the knees; a soiled pink dress cinched tight by a white vinyl belt with hieroglyphics scribbled on it in pink Magic Marker; and below the belt that pink bow. On her head a blond wig and large, square, pink-framed glasses that caused her eyes to swim. There was something wrong with the skin of Miss Buffett's face. She could have been a burn victim, it might have been a disease. The orange meringue makeup was a cracked confection. *Today the voices are an angry throng.*

When Miss Buffett moves, at first the vicar-general thinks she intends to jump into the grave but can't quite bring herself. But then she's pushing past him, and without thinking he reaches for her, to hold her fast, as you would an afflicted child. He's amazed to be doing this, has never touched her before. He is amazed how light she is, how wild, how she flops in his arms like a trout and smells of piss and incense and river mud. He doesn't know what's happening, but what he is feeling is blasting through him like shock fronts, he would fold her in his arms and hold her safe forever if she would let him, but her head has dropped at an odd, intent angle, and she has sunk her teeth into his left hand. His grip springs. She falls sideways, into the grave, landing on the casket like a stuntwoman, crouching, then drops to her hands and knees and, tossing her head from side to side, goes into a kind of wailing in tongues. Immediately one of the cops is down there too, her glasses clatter onto the coffin, and she's out of his grasp, vaulting the straps to the graveside. From there, wig gone, string-haired, balding, the scalp raw-looking, makeup smeared, eyes naked, she is in the air. Her target is the archbishop, who is massive only from the chest up. Mounted and ridden, his legs crumple. Nobody breaks his fall, they step back, he lands hard.

The first cop is struggling out of the grave. The other has skidded in the clay on his heavy scramble round it and gone down. Miss Buffett has the hands of a man. The hair on the back is reddish. The broad thumbs press into the archbishop's windpipe. She is calm but foaming. Intent. She will strangle this monster to death if she can. And then both cops are on her at once, adrenalized enforcers. They yank her off and throw her onto her stomach, a knee in the small of her back, her arms wrenched behind her for cuffing. When the vicar-general begs the officers to go easy, Just back off, Father *he is told by one of them, a truncheon at his sternum.* For a moment, surrounded by the street people, he stands trembling, and then Father Brigilio is walking him away.

‹ ‹ ‹

Later, though the vicar-general has been thinking they have failed to prevent Miss Buffett from being taken into custody and are now driving back to the seminary to do what they can for her from there, *here she is on the seat between them, looking at him.* He holds up his hand to show her the tooth marks and says,

I was in your way.

Is that right, Billy? Father Brigilio says, and reaches for the hand, which he lowers to the seat and grips tight. When was this?

SENSE OF AN ENDING

Micheline was spending the day with her husband's family, at his grandmother's. It was mid-morning, and most
people had fanned out across the fields. There must have
been twelve or fifteen of them, with buckets, moving slowly,
scanning for mushrooms. Micheline was with them, but she
didn't know anything about mushrooms, Walt was out of
sight, and the mosquitoes were biting through her socks.
Mostly when she leaned down she was scratching. And then
everybody was running. Family members there that day she
hadn't seen arrive came rising up in silence over the crests
of hills and materializing out of the woods. When she saw
those closer to her glance around and start to run, she ran
too. Everybody was running back to the house, and she ran
with them. At the house some people ducked in the side

door and disappeared out the front. In the living room one of the sisters was on the phone. Other people didn't even go inside. Five minutes later everybody was jumping into their trucks and roaring off. There had been an accident, a flipped combine at the farm where one of Walt's brothers was helping out a neighbour.

Micheline stayed with the grandmother, who lived with a pair of high-strung Rhodesian Ridgebacks and kept small paper bags of horehound in the dishwasher and old newspapers in the warming oven. Another time Micheline had been there, the grandmother was cooking steaks on a grill on the porch. When one of the dogs snatched a steak from the grill, the grandmother flew to her knees and tore it from its mouth with her teeth. Now, in the night, from her bedroom, the old woman shouted her grandson's name, once. Five minutes later the phone rang. It was the parents. Nobody had known how to reach them. They were on a retreat and hadn't called in ten days. No sooner had Micheline hung up the phone than the dogs started howling, and then the phone rang again. It was Walt, from the hospital.

‹ ‹ ‹

Micheline remembers the pile of turfy mushrooms by the side door. Everybody dumping them as they ran into the house or around to the front. Micheline's own pail sat by itself on the kitchen counter, a third full, half its contents poisonous, as the grandmother pointed out to her, mushroom by mushroom. I guess they don't teach mushrooms at the university, the old woman said. And Micheline thought, This is what you get when you pick according to what you can see of what the person next to you is picking. The person picking next to Micheline was Florrie, one of the cousins. Florrie had a condition that prevented her from seeing any colour except blue. On account of this, or in defiance of it, Florrie wore glasses with blue lenses. Micheline wondered at the blue lenses, but who can say what blue lenses do to a world that's already blue? They certainly didn't compromise Florrie's mushroom-picking ability. Hers were in the pile by the side door, and there were no poisonous ones in it, as the grandmother reminded Micheline, more than once.

Micheline could only nod. It wasn't just the grandmother, it was this family when it got together. In their company she couldn't find a voice of her own, and the ones she could find she had too little control of. She'd make a light joke about Walt that even to her at the time sounded aggrieved and judging. You'd think she was unhappily married, which as far as she could tell she wasn't, particularly, at all.

Just try not to attack me in front of everybody, Walt suggested on the drive home after she'd said something especially hurtful. It makes me think that's the reality and the rest is the aberration. When she told him she hadn't intended what she'd said the way it came out, he said, Sure you did. It's you in that situation. You're like the guy with the severed corpus callosum. Ask him to point and he gives one answer, but orally he gives another. He laughs at something he doesn't know he's been shown, and when asked why he laughed, he gives a plausible reason without knowing he's made it up.

A family operating in harmony was a new experience for Micheline. She doubted the viability of such a thing and feared that to understand this one she would need to take it apart and then she wouldn't be able to put it back together again. Either that or the emotion she would need to set aside if she hoped to fit in would burst out somewhere else and cause damage. Sometimes she wished she could appreciate these people without feeling she had to be one of them, and then she'd remember she already was one, by marriage, and give a little gasp of surprise.

In the family Micheline had grown up in, things had had a way of not coming together or staying put. Her parents didn't drink, but they were always falling down stairs or having car accidents. One or the other was usually on pain-killers or in bandages or a cast. Weekends were dominated by family tasks, which started with everybody in a lethargy of irresolution, escalated to shambles, and petered out. People would agree to take separate vehicles, but somebody would get the time wrong or go to the wrong place or crash on the way. Convinced this was no place to learn how to survive, Micheline moved out to go to university, and today when she visits, her parents' lives are no less on the brink of ruin: their marriage, her mother's health, her father's job, they're losing the house. Micheline's sister got it right when she said to her one day when they were thirteen or fourteen, You know, if this was a horror movie, our family would be the first ones to die. She and Micheline were biological siblings who had been adopted together. The worst thing they could say to each other was, *You* are their biological daughter.

When Micheline was little she assumed that she and her sister were the only people in the world who had thoughts. As an adolescent she'd be in church or at a school assembly or family gathering and it would feel like more than she could bear to spend another second in the company of people so evidently as oblivious as dogs to the absurd and stunning triviality of what they were doing. It took all her strength, which was enormous because she was in a rage, not to leap up and scream, *Fuck this shit!* How this impulse related to subsequent self-destructive impulses such as climbing into Terry Cochrane's car on the night of her fifteenth birthday or not quitting smoking until three years ago, she wasn't sure. A monk who sets himself on fire or a samurai who commits hara-kiri does it on principle. What was hers? People are dumb and I hate myself for being one? That didn't sound right. Most people weren't especially dumb, and she wouldn't have minded being like one of the ones she liked, dumb or not.

‹ ‹ ‹

One day a man called about the brother who died under the combine. He spoke to Stella, who'd first got the news by phone from the hospital. The man explained that the closer he'd come to his birthday the stranger he'd been feeling. He hadn't understood why until that morning, when he read the paper. What at first glance he took for his own obituary was her brother's, who had the same name and had died at the same age he himself was now. Her brother's birthday fell on a different day, but who dies on their birthday? When Stella made an excuse, saying she was on her way out and would have to call him back but didn't, he contacted Florrie, who had recently split up with her boyfriend of three years.

A few weeks later Walt mentioned to Micheline that Florrie and the guy had started dating, and Micheline said,

That's not good.

People find each other, Walt said.

It doesn't bother you that your cousin's sleeping with a man who's assumed your brother's name?

People can have the same name. Florrie's not an unattractive woman. Take off those blue glasses and let down that hair. Reach around and undo that bra —

Oh, be quiet.

Micheline couldn't read what the loss of his brother meant to Walt. The brother was nine years older, so maybe it was like losing a parent when you still have both, as well as two remaining brothers closer to you in age. If Walt was quieter and sat looking out the window more often, it might have been grief or it might have been the flu he caught at the gravesite. In the weeks after the funeral Micheline would think,

Walt's taking it like a man.

But what did that mean?

Florrie can spot a psycho, Walt said now.

Those are those magic glasses she wears, are they?

‹ ‹ ‹

At Thanksgiving, Micheline met Name-stealer. He was the kind you'd date after too long with the person you first started dating when you were too young to be dating anybody. Your judgement is unformed and any change is welcome. Though smart enough not to appear to overcompensate, Name-stealer was obviously the one doing the work in the relationship. The bigger challenge for him must have been winning over Florrie's brothers. They seemed to take to him

well enough, but what did Micheline know about male sar-
casm and male competition? She couldn't read these people.
She couldn't read her own husband when he was with them.
All she knew for sure was that when they were together
they didn't seem entirely at ease until they were doing things
together that they had been doing together since they were
children. Everybody had a role, and the roles were fluid.
They cooked together, the men too. They played baseball
and touch football. They hit flies and shot hoops, the women
too. They played charades. They sang around the piano,
taking turns at the keyboard. If they were birds they would
flock, everybody veering in formation.

For Micheline, being with them was like attending a
Rosh Hashanah dinner. One moment the person next to
you is awkward and friendly and at a bit of a loss, the next
they're singing harmony in Hebrew with everybody at the
table except you. It was like her first time at the theatre
in grade eight, a production of *Salad Days*. Distracted by
details — coughs from the audience like muffled gunshots,
the curtain moving by itself, the actors behaving like geeks
— she couldn't get into the spirit of it. To do that, she'd have
needed to be in the audience, but for her the audience and
everything else was part of the show and she didn't understand any of it. When it was just her and Walt in their own
space she couldn't always read him, but she could get into
the spirit. Not when they were with his family.

As for Name-stealer, he could have been one of them.
From some angles he might have passed for a cousin. But
the fact remained that whether Walt's family was chronically
undiscriminating or congenitally oblivious, it was hosting
someone who insinuates and destroys. Micheline thought of

this kind of person often because she didn't want to be one. Like a climate change denier, she was intent on believing that only egotism could have her thinking she could have any effect here at all.

But when people have invited you in and you consistently hit the wrong notes and are quiet at the wrong times, then there's no one thing you can point to, but the atmosphere has already changed, things are starting to fall apart, and it's a fine line between watching that happen and speeding it along, just to get this over with. Meanwhile, unaware of what they're doing, people keep giving you fresh chances, leaving you room — it's okay, take your time — but it's work for them, what you say when you do say something is fatuous or presuming, because ordinary exchanges are not enough for you, you're compelled to delight and astonish, but that's not what you're doing, you're making them self-conscious. They're not enjoying this. They know and don't know in a way they don't need to think about that you are a threat, and when they're finally rid of your company you won't be invited back. Except you will be, because you're family. And it doesn't matter to them, it isn't anything it would occur to them to worry about, that one of the times you're invited back you'll bring everything down around their ears. That's when, in their shock and distress, they'll know that you were never really one of them. They'll get over the calamity you caused, they're practised at resilience, but a part of you hopes they never will.

Don't worry about it, Walt advised Micheline. Just be yourself. Nobody cares.

If nobody cares, I can be anybody I feel like.

Okay, sure. Take your cue from Name-stealer.

But she was different from Name-stealer. She was a different variety of invasive species. She wouldn't have made a call to the family when a member of it she claimed was her age with her name died on what she claimed was her birthday, because that's what a crazy person does. And when the family member she first contacted didn't call back, she wouldn't contact another and then ask them out on a date. Besides this, she understood that there are different kinds of damage-inflicters and different ways they inflict their damage. One kind that didn't interest her would be the most common: those who couldn't care less whether other people live or die. Another kind that didn't interest her was Name-stealer, whatever pathology profile he fit.

The kind that interested Micheline was the one who loves impersonally, like an artist, from a complicated, inappropriate distance, simultaneously too intimately and from too far away. From the wrong dimension. Proust has a couple who are incapable of evil, they're too self-conscious, too into the aesthetics of it, the drama, they can't get past the trappings. This would be her when it came to anything, including love, but it didn't mean she couldn't be as destructive as a narcissist or a name-stealer. On Halloween the year she turned twelve, walking home from trick-or-treating, feeling like a failure as a vandal, she hauled a pumpkin off a porch and up the ramp of a pedestrian overpass, thinking, Why smash a perfectly good Halloween pumpkin? This wasn't evil, it was stock mischief. These were not reservations sufficient to save a pumpkin.

Last year at a party, Micheline listened to a drunk social worker with a classics degree argue that Plato was right: her clients would be better off without fiction in their lives.

Fiction had them thinking they were the hero of their own story but also its author, whose job it was to ensure that bad things happened to them, to give their life dramatic weight. The more devastating the better. Fiction had taught them an impossible point of view, which they had no right to, which was not in their best interest.

Micheline's reaction to this arrogant diagnosis was hostile. You're talking about bad fiction, she said.

Not necessarily, the social worker said. These people will read anything. They don't know the difference. If there is a difference, the way they read.

Remembering this, Micheline thought, Those clients won't be like Florrie, who's a normal, straightforward person fully capable of acting in her own interest. The blue-lensed glasses look like an affectation, but they'll be prescription. The difference between Florrie and me, Micheline thought, is like the difference between a nurse and an artist. Not that Florrie was a nurse or she was an artist. She'd done arts at university, that's all, and still read books. A nurse has experiences an artist would give her right arm for. But the nurse has them the way a nurse has them, and that's why sick people prefer to have a nurse around. An artist, because she's paying attention to the wrong things, will do harm. Get her the hell out of there. It doesn't matter how nice she is or how hard she's trying, at a fundamental level she's ignorant of the reality of the situation. She's more than in the way, she's a menace.

‹ ‹ ‹

When Florrie started noticing discrepancies in Name-stealer's stories, she broke it off. The next day he showed up at her house before she left for work, smashed her cellphone, ripped the landline out of the wall, and told her he was going to destroy her, starting with her head. That was at 7:20. At nine he took a bathroom break, and Florrie made it to a neighbour, who called 911, but Florrie had already suffered a concussion and a broken wrist.

You were right, Walt told Micheline, as if the more impressive one person's far-sightedness the more excusable an entire family's criminal denial.

But I didn't do anything about it.

I love the way nobody can win with you, Walt said. Not even you.

‹ ‹ ‹

Name-stealer's mother posted his bail, but he didn't show up for the hearing.

So he's still out there, Micheline said when Walt told her.

You don't have to make it sound so dramatic. He won't be the first person to put an unfortunate matter behind him and move on with his life.

At a family gathering at Christmas, Florrie at first appeared unfazed by her experience.

I'm really sorry about what happened, Micheline told her.

I bought a gun, Florrie said. I'm taking lessons. He thinks as long as he doesn't wear blue it'll be like camouflage, but he never really understood my glasses.

Why? Micheline asked quickly. What happens when you wear your glasses?

I still can't see the other colours, but I know what they are.

Micheline nodded, understanding neither how that could work nor what conceivable advantage it offered. What she said was, Please don't risk dealing with him. Crazy people have scary energy.

Florrie took a long time to respond to this advice, long enough for Micheline to wonder if she had heard her. While Florrie failed to respond, she pushed the tip of her tongue, slowly and hard, around the insides of her lips. More than once. It was one of the strangest things Micheline had seen anybody do. And then Florrie said,

Oh, that's okay. I learned my lesson.

Micheline had no idea what this meant

Don't get me wrong, Florrie said. I'll be shooting at his legs. And then she dipped her head and said, mock confidentially, Or maybe a little higher. You know the weird thing? she added. That actually is his name.

That isn't the weird thing, Micheline thought. When Florrie dipped her head, it must have been the whiff of popcorn breath that caused Micheline to say, as if jokey-brightly, So. Seen any good movies lately?

Night of the Hunter, Florrie replied immediately. It was great. Have you seen it?

So, then, Micheline said to Walt on their way home. Florrie. How normal is she, in the context of your family?

Too loaded.

Would any other of your sisters or female cousins have gone on even one date with Name-stealer?

Too hypothetical.
But you know what I'm asking.
Not really.

〈 〈 〈

One day in spring, before the bugs, Micheline and Walt were driving north to open up Walt's family's cottage when they passed a boarded-up highway burger place that had been derelict so long it was now surrounded by grass, which on that day was so green there must have been a recent burn. Upon this lime-green ground was parked a vintage red Ford truck in mint condition. At first Micheline thought the patrician-looking couple frozen in a tableau involving two bright yellow Muskoka chairs were checking out the property for investment purposes. But they were wearing matching royal blue dressing gowns, and the woman was in a wheelchair.

What the hell? Micheline exclaimed, twisting in her seat. What was that?

The folks, Walt said.

What are they — modelling?

Fooling around.

There was no —

They don't need a camera. Or a mirror. They've got each other.

Walt's mother had suffered polio as a child. She now played jazz piano, in a trio. His parents had spent their lives doing battle with a succession of small-town councils on behalf of deceased local artists. Sometimes they would get a statue erected, a plaque up, or a room in the library renamed.

The family was used to receiving hate mail and dead animals on the doorstep. They moved often, from small town to small town.

All that starting over, Micheline said when Walt described his life growing up. A new school in September, and you kids had to fit in all over again.

We didn't worry about it.

You had each other.

Oh no you don't.

‹ ‹ ‹

Name-stealer did come for Florrie, but she shot him dead.

Wow, Micheline said when Walt told her.

Good old Florrie, Walt said, and added, looking at Micheline with genuine admiration, So. Right again.

And again you didn't listen.

Florrie did.

Florrie already knew.

Florrie can take care of herself.

The glasses.

The glasses are not a handicap. Imagine night vision if black was blue.

You don't know that.

Not in practice.

Micheline couldn't be sure whether the more unaccountable thing about Walt's family was their talent for taking disaster in stride or their susceptibility to it. In their solidarity they were insouciant around danger. If she was a ticking bomb, either they didn't know it or they were confident they could clean up any mess she was capable of making.

‹ ‹ ‹

At Florrie's trial, the prosecutor portrayed her as a calculating murderess, but when Florrie took the stand and spoke compellingly of the events that led to Name-stealer's demise — the kicking in her front door, the kicking in her bedroom door, the kicking in her ensuite bathroom door — nobody believed the prosecution. It also helped that Name-stealer had missed a hearing on a charge of assaulting this very woman and then had come after her in her own home, uninvited, with a hunting knife. The only question put by the prosecution that stayed with Micheline was how it happens, if you've taken a firearms course to learn gun safety, your attacker is dead. Between Name-stealer's mother, who wore a too-short red leather skirt and testified on behalf of the deceased with a psychotic half smile, and Florrie, in a new pair of blue glasses like upswept teardrops with a surge of rhinestones that trailed out along the arms, it was hard to know who had more to answer for. Cleverly, Florrie's lawyer used the glasses to portray her problem with colour as a disability.

When the verdict — not guilty: the defensive force used had been proportionate to the threat — was read out, the family rose up as one and cheered. Only Walt's mother, in her wheelchair, and Micheline, to whom it wouldn't have occurred to make a show of emotion in court, remained in their seats.

That night Micheline had a dream involving a downtown Harvey's filled to overflowing with Walt's family. He and Florrie were at the grill, cooking burgers. In a show of rebellion, Micheline had declined to join the family that day in favour of spending it as a *flâneur*, roaming the city. But in the reality of the dream, she wasn't so much a *flâneur* as a street person, being drawn by the smell of cooking meat, tacking diagonally across a busy thoroughfare toward the Harvey's, moving in that damaged person's way of taking rapid, short steps so as not to fall on her face. The grill was right up at the front window, and Micheline remembers raising one hand in the manner of someone calling out an order. I'll have a — she said, and hit the glass hard. Inside, everybody went quiet as the pane reverberated and seemed likely to crack and shatter, while she turned on a heel and continued her tack down the sidewalk but not fast enough to miss the roar of laughter from Harvey's.

Later that same week Micheline and Walt watched a movie on Walt's computer about an oblong plantlike thing like a green flatworm, which moved by flipping itself end over end and consumed things by overlaying them. This plant or worm was psychic, and in its brain-parasite phase it turned the host psychic. In the movie it first infected the hero's dog's brain and then his brain and then the brains of other members of his deeply divided family, which it thereby enabled to work together to fight intergalactic invaders, the reason — we learn at the end — it had come to Earth in the first place.

When the movie was over, Micheline said to Walt, Except the part about saving the world, that was your family.

Not really, Walt said, and turned out the light. In the darkness, already half asleep, he said, Hollywood doesn't do real life.

Sometimes during their fights Walt would accuse Micheline of hiding from life in books. Once he compared her to the person at the awareness conference who spends her time checking her email and texting. I say something about keeping your eyes open, he shouted, and you quote me fucking Krishnamurti!

That happened *one time*! she shouted back. And it was one sentence! One turn of fucking phrase! You're the least conscious person I know! When you're not a mindless cog in that ridiculous family of yours, you have no idea who you are!

But this was itself such a ridiculous thing to say that she couldn't keep a straight face as she said it, which Walt noticed, and then neither of them could keep a straight face, and the fight evaporated.

Do you know *me*? Micheline asked him later, in bed, after they'd made love.

Sometimes. And I sure did just now. *Whew.* He held up a hand. It was trembling.

When Walt was with his family it wasn't witless or impenetrable jokes, it wasn't allusions to events or circumstances from the deep past, it wasn't testy exchanges with harrowing subtexts, it was this aggravating consensus, this baffling congruence of implicit behaviour.

Looking to Walt's parents for clues, Micheline saw a high school principal sort of father, tall and silver-haired, effortlessly urbane and articulate and somewhat theatrical, who lacked only the authority that comes of saying things even marginally relevant to the matter at hand. The boss in the marriage was Walt's mother, who made bold cracks that were funny and dead-on and did not, like Micheline's, register as attention-getting. In many ways Walt's mother was an older, more accomplished, paraplegic version of Micheline. If Walt's father didn't always seem sure which of his daughters-in-law Micheline was, his mother knew exactly. Micheline was the likeliest of the four to become her in forty years, except that one way or another she wouldn't make it, which was regrettable but not really very surprising.

‹ ‹ ‹

When the grandmother was found by one of the cousins partly eaten by her dogs, Micheline said to Walt, No. This is too much. Something's wrong.

Walt shrugged. Every breed's different, every individual dog is different. Fifteen thousand years at least we've been breeding them, and look at the variety. Jackel probably started it. Savannah just went along.

No! Wrong with your family!

Why? We didn't eat her.

You might as well have.

What does that mean?

How's your dad taking it?

Worms, vultures, dogs. Gran was already dead, as the coroner has made clear. By the way, Jerry says we can have our pick.

Of what? The bones?

Of the *dogs*!

I don't want a cannibal dog! Who the hell is Jerry?

One of the grandsons from Gran's other family. Jackel

and Savannah didn't eat a *dog*. A vole that eats a deermouse in a trap is not a cannibal vole.

Women don't have more than one family! How many did she have?

Just the two, as far as we know. Jackel's smarter. Savannah's been in his shadow. She needs a life of her own.

She needs to be put down.

If we took him we'd change his name.

Jekyll.

You mean Hyde. You'd think Jekyll, but the bad guy needs to have the good name, as we ourselves have learned, to our cost. And to his.

The funeral was open casket. The dogs had left the face alone. Out of respect, Walt said.

‹ ‹ ‹

It's in a reader's interest to close down on the meaning as soon as she can. She needs to be able to move on as soon as possible to the next story. If closing down was an old habit with Micheline, it was probably a good thing she never succeeded with Walt's family, because then she would have had to move on. It was also possible, though it would mean something different, that she chose to be baffled by his family rather than simply loving Walt, which she was holding off on doing until it was completely safe to do so, which it never would be. There would always be the fear that she would do something, or something would happen, and she would lose him. But of course you'll lose the one you love, one way or another. It's a primary reason you love them. Walt understood this. He also understood that what you

don't want to do is lose them before you've allowed yourself
to love them, because, contrary to what you might think,
that will mess you up even worse. Especially if at some level
you know that it was you who caused it to happen.

This was as far as Micheline had got when, early one
Sunday morning the September she turned thirty-five, sitting
in the sun in the breakfast nook, she suffered an aneurysm.
Walt had been showering. He came downstairs and found
her slumped sideways, a cup of coffee still steaming on the
table next to her, a biography of Proust on the floor by her
heartbreaking wool slippers. As he waited for the ambu-
lance, Walt did everything he knew to do to bring her back.
But soon after the medics arrived, right there in the kitchen,
they pronounced her dead. For the rest of that black day
Walt did what was necessary. His family was there for solace,
but he was in shock, just doing what was required, and it
wasn't until that night, when he climbed into their bed, that
the grief gathered him up and held him in its stark and generous embrace.

THE DRUG-FRIENDLY HOUSE

I first heard about the drug-friendly house when Julie from three doors down stopped by on her way home from work to check if we were coming to the meeting. When I asked what meeting, she said, Ask Patsy.

Patsy's on a walking tour of Bhutan, I told her. You've caught me in the middle of writing her an email. Maybe she meant to delegate me and forgot. She was pretty frazzled by the time I got her to the airport.

It's about the drug-friendly house, Julie said.

When I just looked at her, she added, impatiently, The one across the street from you.

She was standing on our front porch. I was holding the screen door open wide as if to let her in, but I didn't. Now I pretended to search over her head for a drug-friendly house, but all I could see was the Beringers', which will be a drug-friendly house when the moon falls out of the sky.

So Patsy hasn't said anything, Julie said.

I know the feeling, I said. If you're like me, it's always a surprise when you tell one member of a couple something, and later you mention it to the other and they have no idea what you're talking about. This isn't Patsy and me. We tell each other everything. We're always scraping the bottoms of our respective barrels. And just imagine how much we'll have to talk about when she gets back from Bhutan, even after the hourly texting and the daily blog-length emails and me following her village by village on Google Earth. I can only say that our failure to communicate in this particular instance has come as a real shock.

Julie wasn't listening. She was writing something on a small pad she had taken from her purse. Tearing off the top sheet, she said, Here's the time and place. See you Thursday. Maybe. And she turned and went down the steps.

Thursday! I called. To make sure I wasn't making a mistake, I texted Patsy.

Patsy texted back, If u dnt wnt a Rx hse a x th st thn by al mns go.

‹ ‹ ‹

I got to the Community Centre right on time, but the meeting had already started. Or maybe the dozen or so people sitting around the boardroom-style table under bad fluorescence were just getting to know each other by sharing informal accounts of their experiences pertaining to the drug-friendly house. As I took my seat, Karen, a handsome woman with the sacrificially short hair of a young mother, was saying she lived directly across the street from it — four doors down from us, on the other side of Julie — but her van must have tinted windows. I had never seen her before in my life. She told us how one afternoon last fall she was out on her front lawn with her two kids, three and five, raking leaves, when a guy flew out of the drug-friendly house pursued by two others. They chased him up and down the street, and just when it looked like they'd catch him, he ran over and crouched behind her van, which was parked in her driveway. The other two stopped short and hung back, because she and the kids were standing right there. The guy was down on one knee, breathing hard. What should I do? she asked him. Call me a cab, he said. Karen's cellphone was in her pocket, so she called him a cab. When the cab came, the other two watched him get into it, and then they went back inside the drug-friendly house.

As Karen told her story, her cheeks glowed like apples. Before she could finish, the chair of the meeting, a man in a quilted vest, recognizable to me from his picture in the community newsletter as the president of the neighbourhood association, said, Listen. Don't enable these guys. Next time call 911.

Now Karen's cheeks looked like they'd been slapped. If the chair noticed, he wasn't bothered. He was telling us how he used to live in British Columbia, where he'd attended a series of meetings just like this, called to close down a drug-friendly house. Well, they got the house closed down all right, but it turned out that the guy who organized the meetings was running his own drug-friendly house and was just getting rid of the competition.

For a moment all you heard was the buzzing of the lights. *Why was he telling us this?* We listened closely as he next addressed what he called *the desire expressed by some* to meet with the police and with the owner of the drug-friendly house, who was the aunt of its sole tenant, an unmarried female. Next he provided a confusing account of his interactions over the previous year with the aunt and with the detective sergeant whose job it was to keep an eye on the house. It seemed that the aunt was something of a dragon and the detective sergeant had hundreds of drug-friendly houses on his plate. There was only so much the police could do.

Now I spoke up. I must have been channelling the general discontent with this guy, because my tone was querulous. So we're here, I said, to figure out what to say at a meeting that you want to set up with the aunt and the police —

No! the chair cried. *I* don't want to set up a meeting with anybody! I don't care *what* we do! It's completely up to you people where we go next with this! He looked at us, breathing hard. More quietly he added, I'm just saying it's complicated. The aunt lives in the neighbourhood too. There are thousands of these houses in the city.

Here Karen spoke for the first time since he had smacked her down for not calling 911. Let's get one thing clear, she said. You're just the chair here. My understanding was what *he* said — And she turned and looked down the table at me, and as if surprised to see me still there she added, Who are you, anyway?

For that second, the second that Karen's eyes held mine, for the life of me I could not remember.

It didn't matter. Karen had a larger point to make. This

was that even a nonentity like this guy, who has walked in here out of nowhere, can grasp what this meeting needs to be about. To the chair she said, Your position does not give you a right to tell us what we should or should not do to keep our children safe in our own neighbourhood.

Hey! he said, showing us his palms.

It sounds to me, Karen told him, like you're afraid of the aunt.

Who does also live in the neighbourhood, he reminded her.

And you don't seem to think, Karen continued, that the police can possibly do more than the piss-little they've been doing.

Okay, he said, turning grim. Here's what the police are doing. They're taking your calls. As you know, they've asked you to record the licence numbers of all cars that stop at the house. They get a licence number, they punch it into their computer — he mimed this — seven times out of ten the owner is known to them, five times out of seven he's got a cellphone, three times out of five — bingo! — they know the number.

We nodded. This would be the long arm of the law.

So they call him up, the chair continued, and they say, Look, we know where you've just been. If you realize what's good for you, you won't go back there.

So do they? I asked.

Sometimes, he admitted. My point is, the police are on it. How much manpower do they have? A woman finds herself a few unsavoury friends. The drugs come in, the drugs go out. It's a tinpot operation.

At this, Julie from three doors down said in a trembling voice, I can't believe what I'm hearing. Obviously you have no idea what this has been like for us. Last week I was on my front step writing down a licence number, and this character gets out of his car and comes up my walk completely covered in tattoos and asks me what I'm writing. I told him, my laundry list.

Everybody laughed.

It's not funny! Julie wailed. These guys are *scary*! On an angrier note, to the chair she said, If you're telling me it's the most natural thing in the world when my street turns into a hangout for dopers and criminals, then, mister, you lived in BC too long.

At this, Bob Beringer shouted from the far end of the table, The aunt should put the niece on an acreage, where her druggy pals won't have law-abiding citizens to terrorize!

— only telling you what Detective Sergeant Willmott told me, the chair was saying, talking over Bob. He's spoken to the niece. She's ... not young. Very much ... her own person. Detective Sergeant Willmott says the licence plate information you people are providing is invaluable —

And it hasn't made one goddamn bit of difference, a woman hooked up to oxygen observed in a voice like coarse gravel shifting at the bottom of a copper sink.

He's talked to the aunt, the chair persisted, who might just come around. Our best hope is, the niece herself will understand the situation can't continue. She'll have to close her door to these people or face eviction.

But how long will she be given? a strikingly beautiful woman perhaps seventy-five asked in a voice of polite bewilderment. She wore a charming expression marred only by a look of horror in her eyes that never left them the entire meeting.

When the chair had no answer for her, I saw my chance. So where are we, I asked, with this meeting with the aunt and the police?

Okay, the chair said, coming out of a momentary paralysis caused by the beautiful old woman's question or perhaps by the look in her eyes. With a glance in my general direction, he said, Detective Sergeant Willmott has requested we hold off on that. He's asked us to give him a month. He'll talk to the aunt again, and the niece —

What kind of drugs are we talking about here? a man I sometimes see walking a schnauzer suddenly wanted to know.

To this question, in the manner of one familiar with the blandishments of an altered consciousness, the chair replied dismissively, Oh, the usual. Marijuana. Hashish. Maybe a little ecstasy. Nothing remotely addictive, really.

When people just looked at him, he leaned back in his chair and, like a man luxuriating in the moment, outlined *another route we could go*. We mount a security camera on a street lamp, he said, trained on the house, motion sensitive, and — bingo! — a direct feed to police headquarters.

Would you *please* stop saying bingo, Karen said.

After a short silence, we were addressed by the distinguished gentleman sitting next to the strikingly beautiful old woman, who turned horrified eyes upon him as he spoke. The niece is not an addict, he said. I know the family. She's one of these people who, for one reason or another, have fallen out of step with the way things are generally done. Too much integrity, perhaps. Too . . . giving. I wouldn't be too hard on anyone involved. The narcotics element is a separate issue.

Not if they're being dealt out of a house the aunt owns and the niece lives in it isn't, Julie said.

I am pleased to report that in the end we voted eight to five, with two abstentions from people who hadn't said a word, to give Detective Sergeant Willmott his month.

A motion was made to adjourn.

Bingo! the chair said.

‹ ‹ ‹

That evening, as I made myself a lonely chicken-tender stir-fry, it came to me that the woman in the drug-friendly house must have been the same one who'd appeared in the small hours last summer at our son Cam's twenty-first birthday party. Patsy and I had checked into a hotel for the weekend, and so we missed her, but Cam said she just walked in with her little dog at three in the morning and started clearing glasses and doing dishes, saying things like *Don't mind me* and *You're only young once.* Cam, as drunk as his friends, wasn't sure what to do about her. In the end she stayed, and he was able to blame her for every cigarette burn, carpet stain, and hole punched in the drywall.

The drug-friendly house was a vinyl-sided bungalow un-remarkable from the street except for a weedy firepit and an apple tree out front. For days at a time, a sun-corroded Chev Impala was parked on the brown grass next to the driveway. Sometimes the house pounded like a boom box. One afternoon there was an explosion, too loud to be a gun-shot. Recently in the front window I had seen what looked like an artificial Christmas tree. Christmas was so long ago that it was possible the tree had gone up early. Like stepping out of the night with your dog to clear glasses at a party for twenty-year-olds who don't know who you are, the tree suggested a benign, crackpot domesticity, a willingness to enter into the larger cultural conversation.

It was around this time that I had a dream about a cascade of tectonic events that causes other-dimensional amphibians to leach into materiality and swim the jet stream in search of unconventional thinkers. In the dream, recruiting homeless unconventional thinkers is no problem, but when an unconventional thinker has a roof over their head the difficulty for an other-dimensional amphibian is knowing where the unconventional thinking ends and the house begins, and so it takes the whole house.

I don't know if this dream was inspired more by the drug-friendly house or by the information flowing in daily from Patsy in Bhutan, where fishing is illegal because fish are wild creatures; where society is matrilineal, so old women live with young men and nobody bothers to get married; and where signs say things like *The more you sweat in peace, the less you bleed in war* and

THANK YOU   HAVE COMPASSION
NO TIME TO JOKE WITH AIDS.

It would not have surprised me if the day the amphibians leached back out of materiality, one of them departed with the whole of Bhutan under its arm (more accurately, webbed forelimb), although this scenario was perhaps over-indebted to Patsy's experience as filtered and framed by her enthusiastic reportage.

On a PD day for me, with no vehicle parked out front of the drug-friendly house and all seemingly quiet inside, the drapes standing open, I knocked at the door. As I waited, a cab moved slowly along the street behind me, and already I could see the headline:

DRUG DEAL GONE WRONG:

NEIGHBOURLY HOUSE CALL

ENDS IN FATAL CROSSFIRE.

But the cab continued on until it reached the letter distribution box at the corner. There our mailman got out. He must have been running late. Perhaps he had family money and delivered mail strictly for the exercise and fresh air. But then, why take a cab? Because he could afford to be late? Okay, fine, but what about his health? As he crouched to unlock the box, the door of the drug-friendly house was opened by a lean, wary woman with fine threads of grey along her part. At her feet, an orange Shih Tzu started barking as soon as it saw me.

Hi, I said. You don't know me. I live in that house over there. You pitched in last year with the cleanup at my son Cam's birthday party. Thank you for doing that. Receiving no response, I extended my hand. I'm Morris.

Audrey, she said. We shook hands. Audrey's grip conveyed the concentrated force of multiple small bones.

As for the little dog, it gave one short, sharp yap, spun around twice, shot me a dirty look, and with its rear end in the air and me after it followed its mistress down a brief hallway past a perfectly ordinary living room, Christmas tree just part of the decor, into a kitchen last renovated fifty years ago but clean enough. Dust motes drifted in a ray of morning sun from a window over the sink. As the little dog clicked across the lino to check its bowl, Audrey took a bag of spring greens from the fridge and invited me to look inside.

At first I didn't see anything, and then I did. Blinking up at me from a shallow bed of flat-leafed spinach, the pulse in its throat going but making no sound, was a small, pale green tree frog.

They want me to take it back to the store, Audrey said.

‹ ‹ ‹

She meant the Superstore on Fifty-first. We didn't take the dog. Audrey sat in the passenger seat with the bag on her lap, saying little. When I wordlessly indicated a message I thought she might find of interest, in yellow letters on a portable black message board outside a pet store on Twenty-second —

BABY FERRETS NOW IN —

she made no comment. Inside the Superstore it was a quiet Monday morning. The posture of a young produce stocker examining a grapefruit pyramid suggested a kid with a head full of dreams just putting in time. *Whoa!* he said when he saw the bag in Audrey's hand. He led us through heavy swing doors with rubber bumpers into a refrigerated cinderblock bunker between stacked boxes of produce on pallets toward a dark corner. He threw a switch — *Whhaaah!* he said. On a paint-stained Rast nightstand, there stood a homemade terrarium. If the four or five tree frogs inside were startled by the sudden brightness, the only sign they gave was one slow, asynchronous blink.

Schwumpff! the kid said. This was hardly the sound of a bag of spring greens being emptied into a terrarium, but Audrey was already untwisting the twist-tie. The contents of the bag floated down to make a fresh green carpet, but even as we watched, various sectors of the carpet rustled and heaved, and soon six tree frogs had crawled out to gaze up at us, arranging their tiny thighs, with pulsing throats and not a sound between them.

Ta-*da*! the kid said.

‹ ‹ ‹

Back at Audrey's, the sun-corroded Chev Impala was parked on the grass again, and on a kickstand out front was now a Harley-Davidson. I'll just drop you off, I said, but a look from Audrey let me know I was coming in for coffee. The little dog was overjoyed to have its mistress back. Me it lunged at with a demented yip. At the door to the living room Audrey paused to introduce the three individuals who had made themselves at home while we were out. Wayne and Bo were slumped on the chesterfield, for all the world like two worthless layabouts. More prepossessing was The Organism, a buzz-cut individual in an unbuttoned short-sleeved floral shirt, who sported solid tattooing from his chin to his beltline. Like a speaker reviewing a keynote address, The Organism sat hunched forward in a wing chair, going through a stack of three-by-five file cards.

Hey man, he said when Audrey introduced us. How's it going?

Good, I said. We just dropped off the tree frog.

I don't know what that means, he said.

Here I was tempted to offer a droll account of our trip to the Superstore, but when I looked to Audrey, she and the dog were already on their way to the kitchen. I can explain, I told The Organism. Instead, as if in ironic homage to the disconnectedness of contemporary social interaction, I shrugged and followed Audrey. In the kitchen, the dog was having its topknot fondled while sitting at the table in the lap of a biker, who held my eyes before addressing me by name.

Hey Morrie, long time no see.

We just dropped off the tree frog, I said. I looked to Audrey. She was filling the coffee pot.

The biker extended his hand. Davis Purefoy, he said.

It was a familiar name. As we shook, I told him this.

Fucking I'll say, man! he replied, after a stunned delay of incredulity. You only sat across from me the whole of grade two and half three! Southside Primary, Miss Walser's class! I can't believe you don't remember that. We were best buds!

I do now, I assured him, and I did, except for the last part, but it was too late. Davis was looking at Audrey, and for a moment I thought she must have gone to Southside too. Raising his voice above the tap, Davis said, Sorry, Aud', I meant to add more water, but then I . . . As he trailed off, his gaze drifted back to me.

We had some catching up to do. While Davis touched on some of the good times we'd shared, I reflected that all I'd ever got from Davis Purefoy was knuckle punches and Indian burns. The non-congruence of our memories set me thinking how the human tendency to pass time in unmoored reverie compromises memory as surely as it impedes attention, and I was hardly taking in what Davis was saying. It was only when he mentioned that he'd just done nine months for bottling a cop that I snapped to awareness.

So what about you, Morrie? he asked me. What's your game?

Me? My game? Actually, education, I said, and was appalled by my obvious reluctance to say what my "game" was. How spineless we are! What chameleons!

Still in class, eh bud? And you're thinking to yourself, *Beats jail, loser.*

Not at all —

Davis's world-weary smile indicated that I was not in immediate danger. While the coffee perked and the dog went out of its mind with deranged barking, Davis got me to help him move the table away from the wall. As we fetched more chairs from the living room, he told the others to join us. I said I really needed to be getting along, but Davis's puzzled glance when I said this suggested that he couldn't think why I would want to do that. Audrey set out a plate of cookies and mugs of coffee. When the five of us had taken our seats and got settled, and Audrey had finally sat down with the dog panting on her lap, Davis opened the meeting.

Okay, he said. The way I see it, we have three options: Walk away. Dig in. Open war.

In the ensuing silence I fully expected The Organism to state the only sensible option — *Walk away* — and if for some reason The Organism kept his own counsel, then Wayne or Bo or both together, having no filters, would blurt it out. But this was to fail to appreciate the depth of reluctance of a gang member to appear fearful or cowardly before his peers. Someone "out of the loop" would need to step in.

Open war, I said gruffly. That got their attention. Thinking strategically, like a man possessed, hardly knowing what I was saying, I proceeded to make the case for a *co-ordinated friendliness assault.* There's your drug-friendly house, I said memorably, and then there's your friendly drug house, and which one do you think will still be around in ten years? This means no loud music after 11 p.m. No flipping the bird at the neighbours. All visitors to park discreetly in back. Don't get me wrong, I said. Nothing you do is going to win them over one hundred percent. On the other hand, nothing confuses people like a warm smile. Think of it like living well, only more disturbing.

My point made, and rather well, I thought, I looked around the table. Davis was watching a pencil pass end to end through his fingers. Audrey was retying her dog's topknot. From the look on its face, you could tell it was visualizing the movement of her fingers, and the next time it stopped in front of a mirror it would look at its topknot and vaguely wonder if it could retie it itself, and then it would glance down and notice that it had no fingers, and by that time it would have forgotten this whole sequence of thoughts, if that's what they could be called. Wayne and Bo were engrossed in some kind of rib-elbowing game and in serious need of a time out. Only The Organism showed genuine interest in what I was getting at. What the fuck are you talking about? he inquired thoughtfully.

‹ ‹ ‹

Now for the sad part: they didn't want to know. This became apparent to Patsy and me not a week after she got back. One morning, as we set out on another walk around the neighbourhood from which I would return with Bhutan dribbling out of my ears, we came down our front steps and were brought up short by the sight of a six-foot chain-link fence with barbed wire along the top, entirely surrounding the drug-friendly house. Sometimes you reconnect with someone from your past, and in no time at all they've said or done something that reminds you why it didn't work out the first time. Still, it's a sad commentary when all that comes of an unbuttoned exchange of ideas around a kitchen table is a chain-link barricade. By that time, the aunt had sold the drug-friendly house to what was rumoured to be a numbered company held by a biker gang, and Audrey had moved out, to well beyond the outer limits of the west end, far from the tensions that, despite heroic efforts by the neighbourhood association, working hand in glove with Detective Sergeant Willmott and his men, continue to plague our neighbourhood. I just hope the coyotes don't get her little dog.

Fortunately, my personal interactions with the residents of the drug-friendly house continued happy. So when two officers recently came to the door to ask if my family or I had ever encountered any problems or disturbances from that quarter, I told them uncategorically that we had not. While I can't speak for my neighbours, I said, in my own experience the residents of that house have been *model citizens*. As evidence of this, I mentioned Audrey's helping hand at my son's birthday party. I also asked them to picture a convivial, free-ranging kaffeeklatsch in her homey kitchen on a gloriously sunny morning.

The officers neither affirmed nor denied my favourable assessment. From their body language I would say they tuned out at model citizens.

On a less sanguine note, after the meeting at Audrey's, as an expression, I suppose, of his gratitude for my contribution, Davis insisted I accept two "hits" of what I thought

I heard him say was ecstasy. Now, drugs are hardly my "thing," but Davis's intemperate response to my refusal took me back to one or two occasions when I have inadvertently offended my foreign hosts by declining some grotesque keepsake or disgusting food item. And then I asked myself, Will Davis be any the wiser when they go straight into the trash as soon as I arrive home? In a quick *volte-face*, I cheerfully accepted his gift. But once safe home, I remembered Patsy's fond accounts of her hippie days and forgot it on the mantelpiece, and when she got back from Bhutan and came across it dusting, she seemed intrigued and suggested we "drop" it the first Saturday night we had nothing better to do. Even as every atom of my being screamed *No!*, I readily agreed. What better way to acknowledge the depth of our love than by "dropping" a modern-day "love potion"?

Well, either I had misheard Davis or after my initial refusal he gifted me something completely different, perhaps in the spirit of revenge he'd always been known for. While the lasting effects of Patsy's hippie days seemed to render the poison in her system relatively innocuous, I enjoyed no such advantage. I was soon crouched before the refrigerator in a psychic death grip with a lizard-like raptor obscenely impersonating my wife. When it unexpectedly seized the handle and pointed inside, it's possible it was inviting me to join it in a late night snack, but I could only assume it wanted me to climb in. When I demurred, it canted sideways to open the vegetable drawer, from which it removed a bag of spinach greens. This it tore open and held out to me, with a salacious leer.

Just as when Davis Purefoy had offered me the poison that was even then coursing through my veins, my first impulse was a polite *No thanks.* But this time it seemed imperative to know exactly what I was declining. This must be why I stepped forward and peered into the bag. And there on the green carpet, in a squat, naked but for long, floating orange hair, with a topknot, was a creature into whose heavy-lidded globes my being swiftly poured, then swung round. I shifted my thighs, my throat pulsing, and in a voice hoarse with outrage and yet sounding a note of primordial complacence, I croaked, *Bingo!*

Aw idney koot the giant face above me rumbled, with a lizard grimace.

Bingo! I reiterated.

Wee urr dyoo! the giant face crowed, a look of depravity creasing its scaly features.

Bingo! . . . Bingo!

It was no use. Next we'd be on our way to the Superstore and the kid who spoke exclusively in sound effects. He'd take care of me.

NIGHT DREAMS OF THE WISE

The other day I asked my friend Rudolfo Barrington if things are getting better or worse. He told me worse. I asked him when they'd last been good, which exact years of which decade. He named a three-year period, from the last century.

So in your view that was the high point?

He said it was.

Rudolfo and I are the same age. It was easy to count back to when we were in our early twenties. For most people things were last good when they were in their early twenties. It doesn't matter how good they thought they were at the time.

When I pointed out this correlation to Rudolfo, he said, So?

So in our early twenties we open up to the world. The world responds by opening up to us, and anything is possible. Our windows are wide open.

Mine are wide open now, Rudolfo said.

Really? In our early twenties this information would have had you on the floor.

I don't think so.

Now you're barely listening to what I'm saying. Implications aren't ramifying through your mind, changing everything you thought you knew.

People grow up.

In our early twenties, when a piece of intelligence or new information astonished Rudolfo, he would murmur *Mind . . . broken . . . can't . . .* and fall on the floor. Of course in those days we were pushing the envelope. Drugs, yes. But women too. The women were a peril to everybody's sanity, not just the men's. It was hazardous work. Not everybody stayed the course. Not everybody came back.

‹ ‹ ‹

Chimps and apes are fully adult by age four. *Homo sapiens*, having more to learn, take another two decades. When it came time to leave school and enter the world, I talked my girlfriend Rosemary into joining me on the Grand Tour, hitchhiking through Europe and North Africa. We had just broken up for the second time. We joked this would make or break us. It broke us. I also learned how unready I was for the world. A lack of presence of mind is not an advantage on the street. Neither is a poor grasp of what other people are thinking. I was particularly weak on anybody with a sense of humour. I had a bad habit of mistaking ingratiation and cunning for gaiety and intelligence. It's a wonder we made it home alive.

On our last day in London, Rosemary and I stood just inside the entrance of the Reading Room of the old British Library — at that time located in the heart of the British Museum — and gazed at the blue leather desks radiating from a hub of card catalogues and librarians, at the walls of bookcases rising to a catwalk and beyond, at the skylit dome, and I thought,

Maybe if I read more books.

This became a priority. Three years later I was spending five and a half days a week at Marx's desk in the British Library, reading books.

When not at Marx's desk I was seeing the wonderful Milly Chandos. I say wonderful because Milly was, but also because it was a word she often used. After two years in Gstaad living with the world-famous avant-garde sculptor Laszlo Brückmann, Milly had returned to London to write a book called *The Eternal Helix*. Milly's beauty and birth were such that, even though she had never written a book and hadn't started to write this one, she already had a publisher. Meanwhile she was still turning up helixes, and the more she turned up, the more she found.

It's like elastic bands on the sidewalk, I explained. Once you start to notice them —

No, Milly said. Helixes really are everywhere. It's why I need to write this book.

One evening after a drink at the Plough we were crossing the Museum courtyard, returning to our respective desks, mine Marx's, hers Germaine Greer's. I was telling her about Bishop Berkeley's *Siris*, concerning the purifying virtues of tar water, and she said,

Yes, but does he say anything about helixes?

No, I assured her. Strangely, he doesn't. Not a single helix does he allude to even in passing.

We laughed and walked on. As we started up the main steps to the Museum, I said,

Hold on! Now that I think of it, he does say something about one! An *eternal* one!

And Milly's mind, packed to bursting with helixes, broke. She staggered and fell to her knees on the steps.

God, I loved that woman, but it wasn't working.

She was okay with having me in her bed, preferring me there to not there, but she wasn't ready to make love with me. The day she left him, as he helped her with her bags to the taxi, Laszlo Brückmann had happened to let drop that he would know it every time she had an orgasm. She believed him because whenever she had one on her own, he would call within the hour.

And to make you feel even worse, I asked, does he sometimes wait five or six hours, or even as long as a day or two?

Fuck off, Milly said, wonderfully.

‹ ‹ ‹

One grey morning in Milly's flat in Battersea, south London, she'd left for the Library early to see a man about a helix, and I was moving naked through her rooms. One of the things I'm drawn to at such times is fire. It must be the warmth. As I paused before Milly's gas fireplace, I reflected that, whatever its effects, the reading I was doing at the British Library had resulted in my doing neither fewer foolish things nor things that were less foolish. If anything I was doing more foolish things that were more foolish. To take one example,

I would continue to recommend myself to Milly Chandos, even though — or because — there was no future in it. She was too frustrating. I would not force myself on her any more than I intended at this moment to sear myself at her gas fireplace, but circumstances would need to conspire to end this, because I wasn't going to.

In the days when he would fall on the floor at the slightest provocation, Rudolfo Barrington and his partner Margaux Lemieux and I used to argue about how a person should live. It was our major ongoing point of contention, and still is.

Me: *Know thyself.* Socrates. It's the only advice anybody needs.

Rudolfo: Don't be a sap. Where were you when the civilized world agreed as one that *Anything is possible?* A caterpillar that tried to know itself would never become a butterfly. Gide. Real life can't be plotted. It's noise.

Me: People should watch themselves the way they'd watch a snake at the foot of the bed.

Margaux: To do that you must love snakes.

Me: By watching, you learn to.

Margaux: I hate snakes. Watching a reptile is not freedom. Living for those times *we don't know what we're doing,* that's freedom.

For Rudolfo and Margaux, freedom is orchestrated irresponsibility, arrangements of times out from the terrible nightmare, really, when you think about it, burden of self-consciousness. To them, *Know thyself* sounds like enhanced self-control, and with a view of freedom like theirs, what else could it sound like?

That morning at Milly's fireplace, two things occurred to me. First, wisdom and knowledge are not the same thing.

Second, Know thyself can need a helping hand. If this was the Garden, I still had the old Garden quandary: do the right thing or find out for myself? My policy until now had been to go for the apple, to learn all I could before circumstances conspired. There's the other person to get to know, and then there's you, with them. It's a fine rain of information, emotional, most of it, and it can take months, even years, to soak in fully. I'd assumed that as I grew in knowledge I'd behave less and less like a fool, until I was passing as wise, initially among strangers and the young and naive but eventually, as I grew older, among ever older people, particularly men. Unlike women, who as they age grow more suspicious, men, once they pass fifty, automatically defer to any male stranger at least ten years older who isn't palpably a bum. But now I had to wonder. At the British Library you soon learn that the more you learn the less you know. In London you soon learn that doing the wrong thing can make for a full and interesting life.

I must have been genuinely worried about this and not just looking for a way to feel bad about myself at a time when I had every reason to be happy. At the Library the next day, it was like an eternal helix or sidewalk elastic: in a book about Eastern thought in the Levant in the later Middle Ages, an ancient Chinese proverb did what a key motivating phrase in a book being read by Elmer Fudd or Wile E. Coyote will do. It magnified off the page:

The wise man never dreams.

Wow, I thought, pressed back in my seat by the truth of this. Of course he doesn't.

In my hunger to know how to live I had taken those five words to mean not that the wise don't daydream but that they don't dream when asleep. All I needed to do was figure out how to stop dreaming in the night and I would be wise. It would be the back door, but I would be through it and up the stairs and mixing freely with the illuminati before they knew what was happening.

For weeks I had the British Library book fetchers fetch me every dream research book and article in the Library holdings. As I read, the following scenario came into focus: A squirrel in a tree, going about its day. Suddenly, out of a blue sky, a hawk, talons spread. The squirrel dekes, adrenalin and fear flood its body, it escapes. That night it dreams this moment. Whatever muscles the deke called into play, they must have been the right ones, because the squirrel is alive to dream it.

Dreams, according to my research, are a side effect of extra protein-rich blood flooding up the brain stem to consolidate muscle memory, in preparation for next time. The only way human dreams are different from squirrel dreams is that most of the time for us the hawk is other people, when it's not an inconvenient thought, word, or action of our own. The threat is not to our body but to our self-image. And if we're too tired or distracted to notice it, then whatever had our attention at that moment will show up in the company of an emotionally similar image or memory from our experience in the previous twenty-four hours. But pay attention at the time and there's no need to dream it.

As soon as I'd assembled this house of cards and had it set in stone, I paid a visit to a third-floor office in Soho, where a man with a Beatle or perhaps Jimmy Savile haircut kept a cardboard box under his desk containing devices resembling computer mouses. You held one in your hand,

and when you were having an emotion the changes in your galvanic skin resistance caused it to beep. When I told him I'd been hoping for something more discreet, which I could wear and consult like a wristwatch, he acknowledged that a wrist model was currently in development, but he couldn't tell me when it would be ready. He did say it would cost more and not be as sensitive. So I bought the hand-held one, and when it didn't work at all, I threw myself, every hour of the day I wasn't actually reading books at the British Library, into paying attention to my reactions. Meanwhile in the night I woke every ninety minutes to write out the dream I'd just had, beginning at the end and proceeding backwards. The next morning I typed it all up, annotating as I could the sources of all elements, every detail and scenario, and after eighteen months of this I was recovering 95 percent of the sources of all dream information available every time I woke up.

By then I was no longer seeing the wonderful Milly Chandos, who was making love, or demurring, with the man with the helix, while I was being treated like a throw toy by Doris Gordon, the American wife of Alistair Lovejoy, the British defence secretary. When Doris's and my eyes met across a crowded Damien Hirst reception, her pickled shark and my pickled shark entered into a mind-lock. Doris would call in the night and talk in a low, tough, heavy, driven, tobacco-ravaged voice that left me quaking with excitement and fear. Doris's failure to be like anyone I had ever known was easily enough to win and keep my full attention. For me, the fact that an affair with the wife of the British defence secretary was exemplary fool behaviour and would end badly if not horrifically counted for nothing. To leave now would be like forgiveness without understanding, which as everybody knows but nobody likes to admit is a curse by another name, a smiling fuck you.

Meanwhile, the more aware of my reactions I became the slower they were and the easier they were to catch. Another unexpected development was the continuance of this awareness throughout the night. My dreams were now lucid. Instead of a cognitively impaired dreamer run ragged trying to make sense of a flickering slideshow of anxious moments as if they were real life, my brain simply noted the source of each detail, as it came up, and this in turn made the morning annotations a breeze. After a year, my dreams hadn't gone away, but they were awfully quiet. My waking mind was now so alert and observant that I had forever to respond to everything. The drift and tenor of my actions were still a fool's but a fool confident in the knowledge that he was walking wisdom's path.

I couldn't talk to Doris about any of this. When she was thirteen and fourteen, her pediatric psychiatrist had taken advantage of the couch in his office to introduce her to the full spectrum of male sexual desire, thus ensuring, among other things, that any hint I had a life of my own revealed that I was just another back-door man, and until Doris's heart once more grew fond in my absence, I would be out on my ear yet again — thinking, That's wisdom's back door, my Fury. Just you wait.

On my next trip home, I outlined the results of my dream investigations for Rudolfo Barrington, and his view was that my invasive research method was skewing the data and I was finding what I was expecting to find. You'll never sleep through the night again, he warned me darkly. And added,

Who wants dull dreams? Dreams are the freest, most creative part of most people's lives.

Dreams are anything but free! I said. That's the whole point! They reinforce conditioning! They consolidate neurosis!

Nobody's going to buy it.

Why drag in other people?

Because some day you'll go public with this and embarrass yourself.

Back in London, two or three times a week I was Doris Gordon's escort at functions Alistair was too busy or important to attend. Sex with her afterward, before, or during was like sex with a flash mob. I don't know how common this is, it's probably a well-documented subcategory of acid flashback, but in those days when I made love with a woman her face became a rapid succession of stills of all the people she was, had been, and ever would be. A dream slideshow, random through time. As if that wasn't enough, when Doris made love, she really did become all the people she was, not all of whom were women or resembled her in the slightest. Some didn't even seem to be human, exactly. It was like having sex with a shuffle of creatures from the larger galaxy. Proliferation was also the secret of Doris's brilliance. She occupied every seat around the table. This was why she never lost an argument and never failed to impose her will. She was a remarkable person, but unhappy, lonely, prone to dissociation, and generally adrift, as her involvement with a twenty-four-year-old student will have already suggested.

For my part, I couldn't believe she'd chosen me. I didn't know yet that most men avoid brilliant women, however beautiful, especially the older ones with more than one personality.

But along with having everything to learn, I had never fore-seen an unpromising relationship I didn't want to be part of. All the way back to Desirée Quetico in grade nine, the more love I had to give the worse things had got, and yet still I'd meet a woman fizzy with intelligence, rage, and craziness and think, I can help you with that. You'd think my love was a healing force, and when it wasn't enough, at least it had been a wild ride and I had done my best and knew who to blame.

Doris Gordon was in a league unto herself. One Mon-day, Alistair was in Moscow, it was the maid's and cook's day off, and we were eating in. Maybe the staff were some-where in the house, maybe they weren't. It was a big house. Our meal was leftovers from a consular reception on the weekend, and it's possible the scallops were a little off or I had had too much coke and wine.

What exactly happened I'm not sure. I remember Doris tearing at my clothes when we had sex on the floor, half under the dining room table. I can still hear my shirt but-tons clacking across the marble. Next I was in one of the guest room beds paralyzed with fear as the house heaved and surged with hurricane-force energy. Either a crack team of British agents had entered to assassinate me or Doris was raging through with a loaded gun. She did have a gun. I had seen it once, at the back of one of her bureau drawers, among the sex toys. In my nausea, fever, drunkenness, cok-edness, and/or terror I had no idea how many times Doris burst into the room to pump me full of lead or if she burst in at all. At one point my body dissolved in waves, from the toes up, and that's when I knew that it's true what they say, the apple is Death, especially when you're on the ultimate roller coaster, the one that flies off the rails — and then everything went black.

‹ ‹ ‹

In the morning the room was calm and full of sunshine. Either it had all been a dream of a kind I hadn't experienced in quite a while or I had been murdered in my delirium and woken as somebody else. In any case I was back from death, grateful to be alive. I let myself out before the household was up and walked to the British Library. It was early spring but already warm. Where were the tourists? Was it Sunday? People smiled as they passed. Several called out Good morning, and I loved them for that, and if they didn't mean it, would have said it to anybody, I loved them for being English.

Doris had convinced me that if I left her, my future would be a loveless marriage and dead-end job in a Canadian city where it snows nine months of the year. She'd made me swear that I would never betray her and then mocked my fervent protestations of eternal fidelity. More than once she let me know that if I ever came to the attention of her husband he would have my legs broken. I would never walk the same again.

‹ ‹ ‹

Twenty years later I write these things down and I can't believe I stuck it out so long. What a fool I was. But the thing is, to be able to leave I needed to know enough. I needed to go from believing that any day now things would turn around to knowing that they never would. But I also needed to know that from the moment I knew this, all I'd be hanging around for would be the carrots (though mostly it would be sticks: nothing recommends a carrot like a stick), with no learning possible beyond the limitlessness of my capacity for punishment. But given the state I was in, if I hadn't been watching I could easily have missed the change that comes with knowing that I really did know now that this would never turn around, that left to itself it would end only with death; and that watching and that knowing is wisdom.

Walking across London that morning from the Lovejoy residence to the British Library, I was watching, and that's how I knew that I knew. And this meant that it was no longer too soon to leave Doris Gordon and not too late either, because I knew that I had only just learned this. It didn't matter that I should have done it sooner than this, because I wasn't ready until now. I also knew that the pain would be no less, but when it ended it would end. It wouldn't be the memory of what a nightmare my time with her had been that would have me not doing this sort of thing again, because the memory of how bad it had been would bring with it the memory of how exciting it had also been, and sooner or later I would do it again. The only thing that would have me not taking up with a new version of Doris Gordon was knowing that next time there would be nothing I would need to find out for myself. I had already found out for myself. There would be no more occasion for the dream of things turning around, because I knew — and more to the point, I knew that I knew — that they never would. I would be in it strictly for the carrots and the sticks.

‹ ‹ ‹

But what about you? Rudolfo asked me the other day. When were things last good for you? Those years you spent in London?

When I think that, I assured him, I remember how they actually were, and then I don't think it anymore. It's a good thing I was paying attention. People who assume things used to be better are the ones who weren't paying attention at the time.

I remember everything, Rudolfo said, and trust me, they were better. If they weren't good, they were still better. And by the way. As your friend it's my duty to tell you. This grain-brain philosophy of yours hasn't done you a lick of good. You're exactly the same fool you were the day I met you.

But happily married, I reminded him. Sixteen years next month.

People get lucky.

We're all fools, Margaux said, in the dismissive way someone in the group will get the obvious point out of the way before nailing the one most salient. But then she got up to pour herself another coffee, and when she came back and saw us still sitting waiting, she told us her dream from last night, about walking past the Garden on her way to the dentist and being invited in for a threesome.

Did you go? I asked.

Margaux frowned. I couldn't get the gate open. They threw me a key, but it was plastic, more like a toothbrush. Anyway, they already had the snake.

You hate snakes.

I never dream, Rudolfo said.

WING NIGHT

A ghostly or larval quality about Derek Witten made him difficult to place, or see. Once, at a party, he fell into conversation with a tough Mae West–style professor. Though she started out questioning him closely, she soon eased up and it became a comfortable exchange. But before she sashayed away, she said, I don't know about you, Witten. You don't seem to have any kind of a centre.

It took a Mae West to say it, but many people felt the same about Derek, when he registered at all. Some felt he had the character of a quantum haze: neither this nor that until somebody wanted to know. But given his effect, nobody did. The right kind of attention paid might have snapped him into focus, but such attention is rare. The only thing beautiful Ritu at the IGA ever said to him she said while handing him his Visa slip: *I'll just get you to sign that.* It was a statement of intent, a request, a word of assurance, of advice, of warning, but from Derek it asked no more than a signature that matched the one on his card, which Ritu never even glanced at. Was this because she trusted him implicitly or she couldn't care less whose card he used? As Derek threaded his fingers through the handles of his plastic grocery bags, Ritu would speak the words that marked the end of their exchange: *Have a nice day.* But all Derek could ever think to reply to this sounded like a sullen curse: *Same to you.*

The chat line women were ready to talk, but they soon put aside all interest, sincerity, and ordinary human decency. What was another pathetic creep to them? As for Derek's mechanic, Mickey, like an amiable minor deity he kept Derek's antique Kia on the road, but when they went out for a drink, did Mickey have anything emotionally nourishing to offer Derek?

For several years nothing changed, until one day Derek — by that time a graduate student in engineering at a hallowed, cuts-gutted Canadian university — was chosen by the internationally renowned automotive design expert Laszlo Gauk to serve as his research assistant. For Derek, this was an honour that meant the world. In fact, Dr. Gauk's choice of Derek was owing to an error, but it was a Gettier case. A Gettier case is something you believe is true, and it is, but not in the way you think. For example, you're correct in believing that your wife is having an affair with Jim, but you've got the wrong Jim. This Witten fellow will make an excellent research assistant, Dr. Gauk thought, and Derek did, except Dr. Gauk had mistaken Derek's ghostly, larval quality for the indefinite impression left by a gentleman. But a gentleman accommodates himself to the situation in the name of good manners, whereas ghosts and larvae do it out of desperation to escape their condition.

Laszlo Gauk valued character, but on account of his commitment to Canadian automotive safety, selfless dedication counted with him even more, and Derek had no problem with that. In a decommissioned armoury on a height of land overlooking the campus, Derek was soon working twelve- and thirteen-hour days for Dr. Gauk. His only recreation was laps in the university pool followed by a cold shower. In the armoury he spent most of his time preparing to crash the Gauk Prototype into a reinforced cinder-block wall. While Dr. Gauk, wearing a tweed jacket and leather airman's cap, took up a position behind a console on a plywood dais, Derek ranged freely on foot, videoing the crash and the damage, if any, to the prototype and/or its occupant, a human cadaver. With the sound of a crash still echoing around the armoury, Dr. Gauk would smack his fist into his palm and cry, Good *one*, Derek! Sometimes he would step down from the dais to place a hand on Derek's shoulder and assure him they were very close. Derek knew that Dr. Gauk meant close to achieving their safety design goal, but he also took it the other way.

When not preparing to crash the prototype or writing up damage reports, Derek drove a university van to the morgue to pick up bodies donated to science. In the early days he thought, If only people knew, but soon he was just grateful to have an endless supply. As for the living, the need for a log of the effects of collisions on them took Derek out onto the roads of the city and its environs. He was the guy at the wheel of the unmarked white van that roared up the shoulder, horn going, a self-appointed emergency vehicle. Crash or flip a car and Derek would be right there, crouched with his clipboard, peering in through the exploded window, practically before the wheels had stopped spinning, asking himself, *Would the Gauk Prototype have done any better here, and if not, how might it be modified to have done so?*

Those were heady days. Derek's heart went out to the injured and the dying no less than to the recently deceased. The love he felt was like the love of a hunter for the stag in his sights or a gambler for the losing favourite that was not his favourite. Derek was not a predator, he did what he could, and when the medics arrived he faded into the crowd, something he had no trouble doing. Later, inputting checklists of damage to the living and the dead, he marvelled at the human eagerness to climb behind the wheel of a carbon-fuelled confection of flimsy metal and brittle plastic and drive at high speeds in lanes lacking even guardrails of greased rubber, never mind guide tracks, and he knew that a century from now people would look back on the bizarre fad of automobiles let loose on open tarmac with human drivers and ask, What were they *thinking?*

Sometimes on Sundays and holidays, when Derek stepped out of the armoury for a smoke, he would gaze down on the grid of city streets and think that *auto*-mobile pretty well summed it up, and he would wonder where everybody was going and how badly they needed to get there and what percentage of all this non-workday toing and froing could be classified as animal dashes for freedom. And he wondered how much of it was about sex, about the biological imperative to mate at a distance from home, and therefore to travel out, or, as Brian Wilson so aptly put it, *Round, round get around, I get around.* And Derek came to believe that without sex, or the latent hope of it, there would be much less traffic on the roads. And he thought, People think this is freedom. They think they can go anywhere they feel like. What they forget is they can only go where the road goes. And if they leave their lane, or if there's something in it — a vehicle, a moose, a boulder, a sofa kids have pushed off an overpass, anything of substance they're travelling too fast not to hit — then they can be on their way to a destination they think of as freely chosen while unaware that its primary draw has been a promise of spontaneous sex, however improbable, however ludicrous, however grotesque, but their real destination is more likely to be the morgue.

‹ ‹ ‹

In early July, at the beginning of Derek's second year working for Dr. Gauk, a blanket of heat settled over the city. By noon of each day, even the armoury, normally a cavernous fridge, became a suffocating oven. After lunch the Friday of the second week of this, Dr. Gauk, in his youth an Olympic-class swimmer, proposed an afternoon at the beach. With heat causing the crash-test bodies to decompose with grisly rapidity and the university pool packed with people just standing around cooling off, Derek jumped at the chance.

At the ocean, Derek and Dr. Gauk observed every precaution, but a riptide soon carried them far from shore, and though they knew to swim across the current, they became separated. Growing tired, Derek realized that if he tried to save Dr. Gauk they would both drown. And so he let the old man go. But even as he made this decision, he knew that it would make no difference, that he himself was going to die anyway, not only in this stupid way but in the knowledge that he had just abandoned an old man to drown who had not only placed his full confidence in him but shown him every kindness. And just as Derek was going down for the second time in rage and grief and self-loathing more dreadful than any sea, a random wave deposited Dr. Gauk directly beside him and while it was at it the two of them closer to shore. Grabbing the waistband of the old man's trunks, Derek swam hard, one-armed, until he could kneel, and with his mentor on his back he crawled up the beach and collapsed on the sand.

‹ ‹ ‹

Six weeks later, on a cool, rainy Friday, the heat wave a memory from so long ago it could have happened the summer before, with three months of solid work behind them and a new term about to start, Dr. Gauk proposed a drink in the snug bar in the basement of Graduate Student House. Derek was pleased to know that he was now the old man's trusted colleague, perhaps even his best friend. Hadn't he saved his life? But something was bothering Dr. Gauk, and after some painful small talk he mentioned an illness that he had been treated for a year or so before Derek became his assistant.

It was a growth in the shoulder —

You told me, Derek said quickly. It healed —

Yes, yes, healed. Dr. Gauk shrugged. Our riptide adventure has reminded me how strong a swimmer I was once. It's the marrow, my boy. *Kaput*. Nature has sprung one of her little surprises. When Derek just looked at him, blinking, Dr. Gauk said, You know, in the sea, when we were separated and it was the end for me, I thought how ephemeral our lives. Like a bloom of fungus on an irrigated rock, a passing efflorescence. We come and go in an instant while pretending that we do not. Some of us dedicate our lives to prolonging those of others, so that they might die another way, a little later. But really we do it for ourselves, to bring meaning to our wretchedness.

Derek wondered how wise his own thoughts would have been while drowning if he hadn't been so enraged by the stupid way it was happening and the appalling selfishness of his final act.

In any case, Dr. Gauk continued, after much "soul-searching" (as he called it, using air quotes), he had resolved to fly in, at his own expense, to apply the finishing touches to the Gauk Prototype, the eminent Russian automotive design expert Nestor Szenko.

At this news Derek could only blindly nod. Later he had no memory of the rest of the conversation nor of leaving Graduate Student House nor of the walk home to his attic room in the student ghetto. There the entry on Dr. Gauk's illness in the *Bedside Medical Companion* on the floor by Derek's mattress concluded with serene Hippocratic assurance:

> In one respect you may consider yourself fortunate to have contracted this rare disease. For the most part there will be little pain. If the condition is not already in an advanced stage when diagnosed, and if you respond well to treatment, you can expect to live about six months.

‹ ‹ ‹

On a grey dawn in early December, a Tuesday, Derek climbed into an extravagant pre-Christmas impulse purchase, French driving trousers with deep frontal pleats, and drove the university van to the airport. There Nestor Szenko's time of arrival kept getting pushed back. Flights kept arriving that weren't posted on the board. Derek, gripping the cordon, scanning the arriving passengers, could smell the alcohol on their breaths, a volatile mist. Otherwise, for long stretches, nothing. People stood around aimlessly, avoiding eye contact. To pass the time Derek squeezed into a cement-coloured fibreglass bucket seat and, on a greasy little screen mounted on the armrest, watched a movie about a team of psychologically damaged superheroes. Later he was squeezing out of the seat to drive back to town, to hell with Szenko, when the International Arrivals doors opened and a bald, corpulent man in a green suede suit, spotting the sign with his name on it that Derek was holding, quick-stepped around a baggage cart and came straight for him.

Nice pants, the man muttered as he seized Derek's head and kissed each cheek, twice. Good pleats.

Nestor Szenko had a nose massive with exploded blood vessels and skin the colour and texture of a dew worm in the beam of a worm picker's headlamp. As Derek negotiated the rotting spaghetti of exits from the airport, Szenko astonished him by mentioning, as if it were common international knowledge, the appalling track record of Canadian automotive safety design. When Derek's attempt to counter this view was met by heavy breathing, he glanced over. Szenko was sound asleep. Derek trailed off. Right away

Szenko was back, arguing that it was hardly surprising that Canadian *joie de vivre* should so easily eclipse the international bad joke of Canadian automotive safety design. Canadians were lusty folk and the joke a small one. Derek awaited his chance. When Szenko proceeded to argue that what Canada needed now was an automotive safety designer of international stature, Derek leapt in. Too late. Szenko was out like a light.

This kept happening.

And then, somewhere in the crumbling, septic riot of overpasses erected between the city and the river in the days when hope for the future wasn't so likely to destroy it, the traffic slowed, the way it does for an accident, and by the time it came to a complete halt, Derek, an old hand, knew that the cause was only a few hundred metres ahead, inside the newly refurbished Holger Tunnel, a crash site he had never worked. He glanced over at Szenko. The Russian was slumped forward in his seat like the victim of a high-powered rifle.

As soon as Derek reached the mouth of the Holger Tunnel on foot, he set about picking his way through a thirteen-vehicle pileup, asking himself, *Would the Gauk Prototype have offered any advantage here? And if not, how might it be modified to have done so?*

It must have been the anomalousness of the situation — a major accident in the normally smooth-flowing Holger Tunnel, Derek's first time on foot inside there, Szenko asleep back in the van — but within minutes of entering that smoky burnt-rubber-stinking fluorescent hell of moans, screams, and cries, Derek did something he had never done before: picked up an item at the scene, lying next to a flipped Mini

Cooper convertible with vanity plates that said *UGOGRRL*: a woman's severed hand. The hand, which wore an engagement ring, was clenched, but when Derek turned it over, the fingers opened and from the palm a mouth spoke, saying,

Derek, there are no accidents. There is only everything that has ever happened and everything that ever will or can happen, and it's all right here, all the time. The only reason things are reluctant to go one way and not another is that they are not going anywhere. They are what they are, and we are all a part of them, even those whose lives are spent in denial that this is so. And herein lies freedom. Yours, Derek, is an illusion. The hopes that you have placed in the Gauk Prototype are empty dreams.

A few minutes later, the severed hand deep in the roomy pocket of his new French driving trousers, Derek stumbled out of the Holger Tunnel and into the hot glare of the afternoon sun. Back once more behind the wheel of the van, Szenko still out like a light, the hand silent, Derek sat and stared at the vehicle in front, a Hummer, ridiculous but scary, like a tank.

‹ ‹ ‹

A half-hour later, they were routed down an up-ramp and immediately into the heart of downtown. There the hotel Dr. Gauk had arranged for Szenko's stay turned out to be a seedy flophouse. Derek was pleasantly mortified, but Szenko, who swung back into consciousness the moment they pulled up in front, either failed to notice or knew right away he'd feel at home. He invited Derek up for a drink.

Unfortunately, no one in the lobby, including the crippled bellhop, showed the slightest interest in Szenko's luggage, which fell entirely to Derek, while Szenko went on ahead. By the time Derek staggered into Szenko's room with the last of the bags, the Russian was crouched against the wall with his ear pressed to the base of a pebbled green plastic tumbler. The walls were cardboard, and Derek didn't need a tumbler to hear with perfect clarity a pair of lusty Canadians going at it in the next room.

A minute later Szenko had half filled two of the green tumblers with duty-free vodka and was offering a toast. Canadian, he declared — indicating Derek's new French driving trousers — in place of international-standard automotive design capacity, is capable to be people of enormous passion, including — with a nod toward the next room — *beast without pants!*

Whatever, Derek muttered. He was prickly with sweat, and the muscles of his arms and legs were twitching from all the lifting and carrying.

Over the next hour, the bottle emptying three fingers at a time, Szenko's eyes assumed a bulbous glycerine sheen, while Derek, awash in vodka, felt himself growing ever more luminously sane. Soon Szenko, on any subject except how Derek intended to procure him Canadian citizenship, transformed from a raging alcoholic with pronounced narcoleptic tendencies to an international sophisticate high-handing a local yahoo. Unfortunately for Szenko, Derek had no intention of lifting a finger to secure him Canadian citizenship. Dr. Gauk had said nothing about this. If he had, Derek would have sulked and done what he could. Szenko himself he took pleasure in turning down flat.

How then will Dr. Gauk assist me since you refuse? Szenko wanted to know, irascibly shifting his hams, the elbows of his short arms high on the armrests of an over-stuffed chair that filled more and more of the room the longer they drank. How old is her age? She is unmarried?

These questions, indicating as they did Szenko's ignorance of Dr. Gauk's gender, caused Derek to drift out behind an enigmatic smile that sent Szenko into a fury of armrest pounding, which resulted in a half century of beast dust rising into the air for illumination by a mammoth blood-red sun just then sinking into the river. So she swings or she does not, you dolt Canadian? Szenko shouted. Speak! speak! curse you!

Next door, like a rage-triggered oscillator in a nightmare, Beast Without Pants was back at it.

Don't you know even this, you *pleated idiot*? Szenko shrieked.

That did it. *Stop talking about my pants!* Derek shouted.

I speak of nothing else, Szenko countered craftily, until you tell me this: she is or she is not *swinger*?

But all that last word served to do was fix Derek's attention on the chandelier, its multicoloured plastic spikes blackly furred with dust, *swinging* on its furred braid cord from the stipple-and-nicotine ceiling, which along with the floors and walls was vibrating to the rhythm of a renewed *huh huh huh huh* from Beast Without Pants, a headboard lightly slamming.

The phone rang. Szenko snatched at it. Derek heard the desk clerk say something unintelligible. Szenko smashed down the receiver and rushed into the bathroom with one arm high in the sleeve of his suede jacket. Seconds later he emerged wearing an orange pompadour with glistening fibres. Pinching and tugging at his cheeks, he paced. When the knock came, he spun, paused, checked the hang of the jacket in a largely unsilvered mirror, fluttered at his wig with stubby fingers, and flung open the door, crying, even as he started back,

Dr. Gau-Gauk! We meet at last! How *fantastic* to see you!

Szenko, Dr. Gauk observed neutrally, shuffling past him into the room, his eyes going directly to Derek's, each of which was spinning like a caster on a shopping cart.

Dr. Gauk! Szenko cried again, lunging forward. Your work has been inspiration! A pause then. In a confused way, Szenko was looking behind him. His heels had remained stuck, like cleats in a grate. His arms were windmilling. At this juncture, the male component of Beast Without Pants introjected a strangled bray of consummation, while Derek, now on his feet and swaying too, greeted Dr. Gauk with a breathy *Hhh-ahhy* and a toss of his head that sent it straight to the floor.

Time to eat. Dr. Gauk led them to a demoralized second-floor Japanese restaurant at the foot of Flintlock Hill. According to the sandwich board out front, it was Wing Night Tuesday. Each needed help on the stairs but had only the others.

The restaurant offered screened cubicles with raised floors and a hole sunk under the table so that — as in the old Russian proverb, which Szenko now repeated to a glazed stare from Derek — you can sit on floor and dangle feet over edge! The restaurant made good its sandwich-board promise by offering a terrific deal on teriyaki-style chicken wings, a menu item that made perfect sense at the time.

Soon Szenko and Dr. Gauk were engaged in a thrust-and-parry academic debate concerning technical first principles of automotive safety design. Derek took the opportunity to crawl under the table with his teriyaki wings, grateful for the ease of motion afforded by the roomy cut of his new French driving trousers.

After what seemed at the same time no more than a few seconds and an eternity, Dr. Gauk was poking at Derek with his cane. Szenko has requested a demonstration of our prototype tonight. I am a little tired. Would you mind?

Not at all. If Derek's intention was biting irony, his words came out slurred but otherwise civil. He rubbed hard at his face.

A moment later Dr. Gauk leaned down again. Why does he keep falling asleep?

Naked aggression.

After hailing a cab for Dr. Gauk, who even before they reached the bottom of the stairs seemed to have left them, Derek and Szenko made the arduous trek up Flintlock Hill to the old armoury. The night was drizzling and bleak. A sound of distant foghorns. The climb appeared to sober Szenko, who, breathing noisily, retreated into his thoughts.

Derek was unlocking the hatch-sized people-entrance inset in the massive oak doors designed to accommodate military vehicles when Szenko, slouched against the wall, muttered, I always thought L. Gauk is woman. Leda, Lola, Lily — He is ill? His position will "open up"?

Ignoring this, Derek kept his eyes on the giant combination lock cradled in his trembling hands. A moment later he stepped over the sill of the smaller door. For him now it was the cement-dust workplace-familiar smell. In the faint light from the docks that came through the high, squat panes, the interior was a gulf of shadow and silence that sucked at the squeal of hinges and at Szenko's uncertain footsteps behind him. And then Derek hit the switch, and the overhead arcs came crackling on, and the place was right there, as ever, it could have been first thing Monday morning.

Self-conscious for some reason when he reached the prototype, Derek removed the tarp, which he set about carefully folding. This task completed, he turned to see Szenko inspecting the prototype. Stealing ideas, Derek assumed.

But what Szenko murmured was, Surely he jokes. Is — lightly touching the frame — nothing. Is two, three years before. He is kidding himself here.

Szenko looked at Derek with an expression something like pity. In Poland only they are not so far along. The illness has made him — ? Szenko tapped sadly at his temple.

Derek turned from Szenko to the prototype. At first he imagined himself replacing the tarp and walking home. Let Szenko find his own damn way out. Instead, he walked over to the console. From there he explained the controls, which were simple, to Szenko, who was not. And then he climbed into the prototype and strapped himself in.

Under Szenko's operation, the vehicle backed up slowly, about thirty metres.

What speed do you advise? Szenko asked shyly.

Your pleasure.

A low one, in that event.

It works, Szenko, Derek said. It's ready to go. It doesn't need your goddamn "finishing touches." It's the greatest thing since airbags. I'm surprised you can't see that. *Hit it!*

With a jerk the prototype started for the reinforced cinder-block wall, at about fifteen kilometres per hour.

Hit it! Derek screamed.

The speed of the contraption had increased to perhaps twenty kilometres by the time the wall stopped it dead.

Szenko hurried over.

Look, I'm fine, Derek muttered impatiently. I say now we really put it to the test.

Szenko's hand passed across his eyes. Perhaps you will take me now back to my ho — He was fast asleep, slumped against the prototype. Derek unfastened himself, climbed out, dragged Szenko to one side, flipped four toggles, fastened himself back in. He reached under the seat to press several more buttons. This time the prototype backed up forty metres and stopped. Now Derek checked all straps, ties, buckles, and cinches. Satisfied, he slid a needle indicator to sixty.

Being electric, the prototype took its time to build up speed. In fact, Derek was approaching the wall at only forty, maximum forty-two or -three kilometres per hour. Still, it's quite a clip at which to hit a reinforced cinder-block wall.

Once, not long before he became Dr. Gauk's assistant, Derek was following two car lengths behind a young woman driving slowly across one of the great iron suspension bridges over the river. The surface of the bridge was coated in ice, and when the young woman applied the brakes, her car drifted smoothly leftward into the iron railing there, which peeled away its front fender like tinfoil. Very slowly then, the car ricocheted to the opposite railing, which did the same to its rear fender before returning the car to the first railing, which tore off its front bumper, and so on down the length of the bridge. It was as if that young woman's car were made of the flimsiest material known to man, and the parts just kept peeling away, pieces flying off onto the roadway, some first wafting slowly upward before slowly descending. When, finally, the car stopped moving, the young woman remained sitting, hands gripping the wheel, helpless and exposed, a fawn in a go-kart, and Derek, who had watched it all, from beginning to end, left his own vehicle to tower above her in her trembling state, and deep down inside him were feelings like many small things unborn, shifting their thighs.

As for Derek in the prototype, his body, not being dead weight, behaved differently from a cadaver's, or perhaps the prototype had rammed the wall one too many times, but there was a kind of collapse of the right forward bumper assembly, and this resulted not so much in Derek's being squashed like a bug in a crinkum-crankum of buckled steel and reinforced cinder block as his life being saved by the intelligence of design and pure engineering genius of Laszlo Gauk's prototype, inside which his body, though contused, semi-gored, and concussed, remained suspended and essentially uncrushed amidst a crinkum-crankum of buckled steel and reinforced cinder block.

The French driving trousers with the deep frontal pleats were, however, ruined in an unexpected way. All material with the exception of the inward half of the sleeve of the right pocket had been sliced clean away, to leave balanced on Derek's otherwise naked thigh, on a bloodied patch of pocket, the severed hand from the Holger Tunnel, and as Derek returned to consciousness his eyes fell first on this, and in his dream of shock the fingers opened and the mouth said,

Tell him.

As Derek later understood, Szenko eventually awoke and stumbled away. From the airport he first called Laszlo

Gauk, who seemed to have difficulty understanding what Szenko was saying, and second the fire department, who used a jaws of life to prise Derek out. By ten o'clock the next morning, Nestor Szenko was slumped in his seatbelt on the 7:15 Aeroflot flight to Moscow and Derek was resting comfortably in the university hospital.

Visiting hours didn't start until noon, but shortly before eleven Derek opened his eyes and there at his bedside was Laszlo Gauk, saying nothing, only reaching for Derek's nearer hand with a fierce cold grip, a miracle of will, because four hours earlier a wall of blood had breached a barrier in his brain and been seeping through. By the time he arrived at Derek's bedside, though he probably still knew where he was and whom he had come to see, Laszlo Gauk was no longer capable of speech. And so Derek, unable to pretend there was nothing wrong, rang for a nurse and while he waited allowed his hand to be held. And because it was some time before anyone bothered to answer, the nurses being understaffed and burned out and aware that Derek's condition was not critical and that he had arrived holding a severed female hand, Laszlo Gauk folded forward from the waist and rested his head on Derek's chest.

Derek placed his arm around the old man's shoulders and told him how the Gauk Protoype had saved his life and detailed two or three noteworthy ideas for its improvement that had come to him as he was being prised out, as well as a couple of things that had come to him earlier, in the Holger Tunnel, and complained what a miserable disappointment Szenko had turned out to be, but what can a drunken charlatan be expected to know about automotive safety design? and how they must take the long view and live for the day when Canadians would have the courage of their own convictions and stop looking for affirmation from international clowns and second-raters.

And so on.

But really it didn't matter what Derek said, even if Laszlo Gauk understood him, which he may or may not have, because none of it was to the point, as the severed hand, had it not been distracted by a rough ride to Forensics in a lead-lined envelope, would have let him know sooner than it did. And even if Laszlo Gauk had been able to understand Derek pretty well when Derek started talking, he was probably understanding him less well by the time an orderly lifted him into a wheelchair to take him to a ward on a higher floor. But at midnight Derek bolted up out of a dream of riding in an elevator to see the old man, and before he could dismiss this as foolish or sentimental, something — probably the hand, communicating from Forensics — told him that unless he planned to end up as just another lost disciple cinched tight in a fantasy of flesh and safety who was nevertheless in the same fast lane to extinction as everybody else, he needed to do it now. And so, that same night, Derek rode the elevator up to Laszlo Gauk's ward. There, squeezing the old man's icy hand, he told him of his decision to allow him to drown because he couldn't save them both, and though it was true that he had only saved him because he could, that didn't mean — that didn't mean —

Meanwhile, down in Forensics, the hand, absently turning the ring on its finger, observed, half to itself, *People think death wins, but death is only the end of life. Death is nothing, it is less than life. It is far less. It is nothing.*

Tears streaming, Derek murmured, That's right, Hand. And he went on to tell Dr. Gauk what choosing not to save him didn't mean, and he would have done this anyway, but the hand was peremptory, because time was running out.

Tell it to Laszlo, Derek, the hand said. *Tell the living. Tell him* now. *Let him be the first.*

WE DON'T NEED TO HAVE THIS CONVERSATION NOW

Yesterday my friend Dede the tattoo artist spent nine hours removing a labial tattoo. Now that her customer was twenty she was thinking better of something she'd had done when she was sixteen and acting out. But staring at those labia for nine hours burned the image of them into Dede's brain. It was like a jingle she couldn't get out of her head.

A jingle'd be a meme, I said. I don't know about labia.

I don't know what you're talking about.

Brazilian?

Latvian, I think. Why?

I never think about labia, my father said when I told him about Dede's occupational hazard. Not as such. I think about the woman. And I don't get the shaving bit. If you ask me, it's kiddie stuff. But what do I know. I don't even own a computer.

I think about Suzie's face, I told him, when I reach down and draw my thumbnail lightly but firmly along the seam at the crotch of her jeans.

Too much information, my father said. He said he used to pride himself on knowing the score. Now he thinks of that as just an idea he had about himself.

Most of the things people do that get attention, he said, are nothing but ideas. Now when he hears about a new scheme to save the world, he thinks, But that's just an idea. He no longer believes nor is interested in most things he always believed and took an interest in. His illusions have come apart at the seams and fallen away.

Leaving you the man you always were.

No. Picking through the ruins. Now and then turning over something that looks familiar and thinking, What a dope I was then.

Everybody was a fool yesterday.

That's because to be a fool you need to be a double fool. A fool can't know he's a fool.

Until tomorrow, when he used to be.

That's right. He still doesn't know. But there's comfort in that. I'm saying I lost the comfort.

We had such conversations at the Extended Care in Belleville. One day Dede called to say that our friend Ivy Helmholtz, the writer, was in there too. She'd had a fall.

The next time I visited my father, I visited Ivy. She was standing by her bed, with a walker. What happened? I asked.

You won't believe this, she said. She'd been at a poetry reading, the only female in a group of writers at the back of the hall, passing around a bottle of Scotch. There were three readers. The first and second read long, but that was from inexperience. The third was a po-biz veteran known for being put into an incantatory trance by the proximity of a mic. By the time she'd read forty minutes past her allotted time her voice was a fat old golden retriever on its back with its legs spread, having its belly scratched. Ivy was trapped at the end of an aisle. When she couldn't take any more, she whispered that she was leaving by the window. The writers who heard her responded merrily, with air kisses and *Ciao*. They thought she was kidding. It wasn't until she pushed herself off the sill that she remembered the winding staircase they'd climbed, already drunk, to reach the reading. It was a second-storey window.

Sometimes you just have to get out of there, I said.

Ivy's guffaw reminded me how much I liked her. And then another visitor arrived, and I remembered why I didn't see her all that much. She made herself too available to those out-of-touch-with-themselves people who fasten like bloodsucking leeches to the misfortunes and emotional distress of others. At Extended Care they arrived in waves. Singles and couples and small groups. On nice days Ivy would take everybody out to a bench at the bottom of the facility garden, where they could all smoke dope and not bother the other residents. I sat out there a couple of times, but there was something wrong with Ivy's energy. At first I thought it was the dope on top of the painkillers, and then I wondered if physical trauma or even a hospital stay can cause a state of nervous elation. When I asked Suzie, she said,

Ivy still lives alone? Eking out a living as a writer? A woman almost fifty with both parents dead and no kids? Being taken care of for once in her adult life? With daily visitors she can go out into the garden and smoke dope with? What's not to be elated about?

But Ivy had broken several bones, she would be left with a limp, and Suzie hadn't seen her in years. The last time was at a women's solstice celebration a decade before this, where the dope was so strong that Suzie couldn't follow what anybody was saying. At one point, after they did runes and performed other soothsaying ceremonies, everybody wrote down on a slip of paper a habit or a thought pattern she wanted rid of and burnt it. Suzie looked around her at the circle of hopeful, ageing faces and thought, I'm too old for this.

On the days Suzie came with me to visit my father, we also visited Ivy. On our third or fourth visit, Ivy tried to read us a poem she'd written about us all then and now. It was a play on the Dylan line *We thought we could live forever in fun*. But she couldn't finish. She kept breaking down and then laughing through her tears.

On the way home, Suzie said, It's nice the way your friends really seem to like you.

I don't know Ivy all that well, I reminded her. I only slept with her once, and that was twenty-five years ago. She's in a state of unnatural euphoria.

Sometimes Ivy would take her walker to visit my father.

She's a smart woman, he told me, but she needs to turn her damper down.

Most days my father's mind was as sharp as ever, but when he hadn't slept well or was upset about something or was running a fever or his medication was even slightly off, he would lose track of who and where he was. One day he asked Suzie and me to move in closer. To show his appreciation, he said, for the strength of character we'd shown since coming to Canada and as a promise that from now on things were going to be better, he had a small gift for each of us. But when he looked around for these gifts and couldn't find them, he wasn't bothered. He shook his head and glanced toward the window, smiling, as if he might be wrong about the gifts but not about the strength of character we'd shown.

From family stories I knew the speech was one my grandfather had made to his wife and three children on their first anniversary in Canada, when my father, one of the three, was five years old.

When Suzie asked me how I'll do when my father dies, I told her, I don't know. He's old. He's in and out of pain. His mind's going. For sure I'll be sad, but even with him and my brother gone, I'll still have somebody in the world I can trust.

Because you know I won't betray you, Suzie said.

How did you know that?

After Ivy got out of Extended Care, I kept in touch with her at home. One day she told me she had just got back from a meeting with her publisher in his office in an industrial strip mall outside Toronto. After removing from a filing cabinet a series of zip-lock bags packed with sandwiches and salad, as well as a small Tetra Pak of mango juice, he proceeded to eat his lunch while telling her that her new work was too pleasing to the reader and dealt only with the surfaces of things. For these reasons he was unable to publish it. But if it was any consolation, in the course of his career he had rejected two Governor General's and a Giller winner, about whose work he had said exactly the same thing. Having finished his lunch, he washed his hands and showed her a mock-up of the lead book on his fall list. It was called *Moonlight on My Hatbrim*. He also showed her the manuscript, in which Ivy could clearly see the *i*s and *j*s dotted with Happy Faces. He told her that by all indications *Moonlight on My Hatbrim* would be a big seller, perhaps his biggest yet, but on principle, no matter how fast the initial print run of five hundred sold, there would be no second printing.

What principle? wondered Ivy, who was still reeling from his rejection of her new work.

Prudence, he told her. The watchword of the successful Canadian publisher.

When we were younger, Ivy used to say how easily she could end up a bag lady. This was a common sentiment among the women I knew then, a most un-bag-lady-like crew, and I didn't think much about it. But when Ivy's crash came, I would say she went to a place the bag ladies know well.

One day at Extended Care, I ran into Dede, looking frazzled.

Labia slow to fade? I said.

I'm here to see Ivy.

Ivy's been home two months —

No, she's in the psych ward, which I can't find.

This is terrible.

I know. When I heard, I cried and cried.

For Ivy — ?

No, for me. Here I thought for once I had a stable friend.

‹ ‹ ‹

I visited Ivy the next day. The psych ward was a building unto itself, across the street. There every table, chair, bed, wall surface, and floor tile had been carefully selected to crush the will to live. Talking to Ivy was like talking to a desolate child at the bottom of a well. It was like talking to my brother after the virus stripped him of every vestige of his character, and what remained was the serious, intelligent person who'd been under all that personality the whole time. With Ivy, the disturbing energy was gone, and in its place was the mind that had shaped the work on the page, that was not concerned to please anybody but itself, that dealt with the surfaces of things because that's how you come at the rest.

She was hard to talk to.

She told me she felt she'd lost the part of herself that made her human.

Ivy, that's the depression. I said this more than once because I knew it was true. But I also knew that Ivy Helmholtz was not one to hand off responsibility for her thoughts. Not when they were going well and not when they were not.

I told her she had to get better, for the sake of all the people who loved her.

Thanks, she said, but at the moment I can't imagine why anybody would do that.

Ivy! For a hundred reasons! A thousand!

And then I didn't know what else to say. This was not the kind of conversation we tended to have. It didn't go with who we'd always been with each other. Ivy's discomfort talking about herself was part of what drew people to her: she would listen to their problems, she would tell stories on herself and about other people. She did not deal in advice or analysis. And she was not interested in being praised. Her work, sure. Herself, never.

She asked me how my father was doing.

I said my father was doing okay, considering.

She asked me if I'd been talking to Dede.

I said I'd been talking to Dede.

She didn't say anything. And then she said, I'm really tired.

On my way back through the main hospital building, I saw a grey-faced woman in labour being wheeled into an operating room as her husband or boyfriend came rushing in the opposite direction muttering *Got to check on my car.*

At home I said to Suzie, She needs to talk to somebody.

She's not ready to talk, Suzie said. You have to be well enough to talk. They should have her in a group. She can listen to other people talk. Realize, hopefully, she's not alone in this.

One day things are great, the next it's here come the firemen. I'm not a fool today because of how clear it is to me what a fool I was yesterday. There has to be a better way through life than this amnesiac second-guessing. If there is, I haven't found it. But nine weeks later I had a dream, which ended with a sequence involving a bunch of us in some kind of overgrown garden. Beyond the garden was a great house with many locked rooms. In the dream, Ivy and I climbed onto the roof. When I jumped I landed in the sea. When Ivy jumped she landed on rocks. I climbed out to go to her, and she was curled on her side, like a child. I picked her up to hold her in my arms, but she was still shrinking. Next I was cupping her in my hands, but then I was watching helplessly as she grew smaller and fainter, until she disappeared.

When I woke up, I wouldn't say I knew something was wrong, but I did know where the house and garden had come from. It was in a house like that that Ivy and I had made love, on a summer afternoon, in a locked room, during a garden party we were both at with other people. I remember it was near Stratford, Ontario, because we had all been to see *Julius Caesar*, and as a surprise the actor who had played Julius Caesar showed up at the party, and he was an irritating guy, full of himself, a disappointment after the figure he'd cut onstage. He spoiled everybody's memory of a perfectly good production.

Anyway, I knew I hadn't thought about any of this for years. It could have happened in another life, to somebody else. Before I saw Ivy that first day at Extended Care, if you'd asked me if I'd ever slept with her, I'd have had to think for a moment. It's strange that you can be inside a person's body, or have somebody in yours, and later it can mean so little. You'd think an act that intimate would add up to something, but it doesn't seem to. You see a picture in the paper of a high court judge, and you think, That woman once had an orgasm on my face, then swung round on one knee and blew me, and it doesn't mean a thing. It's too much information, even for yourself. It's like a joke that works by surprise, a throwaway line, an inappropriate detail to bring up, at any time. It was just something the two of you did, that people do. There are always other, more important things going on, for everybody, and that's what doesn't go away. Am I the last to be getting this?

Ivy was out of hospital by then, at her own insistence. Before they let her go, they made her sign a statement promising that she wouldn't — in her words — *do myself in*. As soon as I thought she'd be awake the morning after I had my dream, I called her apartment. I'd talked to her only the day before, and she'd sounded okay, not ready yet to meet me for coffee but okay. Now there was no answer, but she often waited to hear who it was before picking up or not, which would also depend on how she was feeling, but as soon as I put down the receiver my phone rang. It was Dede. Ivy had fallen from her twenty-third-floor balcony.

She didn't fall, I said.

Who do you think you're talking to?

When I told my father about Ivy, he said,

The poor woman.

When I told him about my dream, he said,

I had a dream like that the night your brother died. We were on a mountain and I jumped. So he did. But he didn't make it. When I picked him up, he shrank to nothing in my hands. But later he'd drop in on my dreams. There was no story, no agenda, nothing I was supposed to do, or should have done. When I asked him, he told me he just wanted to be there.

My father looked at me. I'll do the same for you, he said, if you want. It'll be up to you. Before I could say anything, he looked away, toward the window. We don't need to have this conversation now, he said. I'm sorry about your lady friend.

The other person in my father's hospital room was a man perhaps sixty. He didn't look well, but according to my father he'd be out before too long. One day when I was there, a young woman came to see him. From the quiet way she spoke to him and from the steady way she had of taking everything in, she struck me as even more intelligent than she was beautiful. I thought she must be his daughter, until I heard him say that she should come with him sometime to meet his friend The Buzzard. He's like me, he told her, another rich kid gone wrong. This is a guy who doesn't care about anything. Everything's a laugh to The Buzzard.

I couldn't make out the young woman's reply, but it was clear that she was not one to put off not being a fool until tomorrow. She had no interest whatsoever in being taken to meet The Buzzard.

FIST FIGHT AT THE ORGY

In late August, under a white sky, fumes of diesel on the dawn air, I tied up at the mouth of the Humber River and walked the Carrying-Place Trail north, as I did every year at that time, when the promise of summer was over before summer was over and the heat-hammered desolation of the city reminded me once again that I had not stopped living in fear of losing life — the lived. And so I walked, because everyone who had ever got to me, for good or ill, the living and the dead, was lodged in my muscles, and walking set each in motion, like a weather front, and better the stately succession of habitation by others than the crying jags that used to leave me exhausted and immobilized well into September.

But on that particular August day everything changed for me, for reasons and in ways I could not comprehend at the time, and this is why, that night, back at my boat, I lit the lamp and made a few notes. It was like coming up half asleep on one elbow for a pen and pad to record a dream in the dark, backwards from the moment of surfacing and so all the way to the beginning of the dream and from there to the end of the one before it, and so on back, remembering as you go, in the knowledge that if you weren't doing this, then everything would be — as usual — lost, emptied to husks and ciphers.

A dream, like memory, is a story we tell ourselves. There is the story and what it means to the dreamer, and then there is what it means to the one who has dreamt it. There are the people in your life, past and present, and then there is what they mean to you — hero, beloved, friend — and when what they mean to you changes, everything changes. After a year of struggle to convey how it came to be that on that one day in August everything changed for me, I had half a liquor box of notes under the bed in my apartment — for I no longer lived on my boat, which I had sold in consequence of that day — and these notes, winnowed to a few dozen pages, became the working draft for what follows.

‹ ‹ ‹

The Carrying-Place Trail soon passes under Lakeshore Boulevard and, a few dozen steps farther on, the Gardiner Expressway. The ground beneath the Gardiner is an artful civic terrain of small boulders set in concrete to discourage encampments by Native and other street people. Overhead, the expressway slabs meet imperfectly, at different heights, causing the road above to make a sudden dip, twenty or thirty metres beyond where, in the fall of '92 and winter of '93, when I was commuting to school in the back seat of a Bentley driven by Mr. Powell, the morning traffic most often came to its first complete halt. One moment we'd be moving along at a good clip, the next it was stop-and-go and I knew I'd be late for school yet again. When I climbed out of the Bentley at the entrance to the parking lot next to Mr. Powell's office at Adelaide and Spadina, it would be anywhere from eight-thirty to five to nine, with my first class at nine, and I still had the Spadina streetcar to catch. Some months in the year I rode with Mr. Powell, I was late for school twelve or thirteen times.

While I remember my gratitude for the privilege of riding with Mr. Powell and the close connection between this feeling and the relief of being assured by my mother that Mr. Powell had once again been heard to say that he was thinking of making an earlier start, I also remember the disappointment and sense of helplessness I experienced each time I knew that I would be late again, and the connection in turn between this feeling and the one that came with knowing that I had no alternative but to ride with Mr. Powell, who didn't even pick me up at my door. Instead, at twenty past seven each weekday morning, my mother and I would leave the house, and she would drive me the ten blocks down Kipling Avenue to Highway 7. There, on the shoulder of the highway, balancing on my hip my giant, massively heavy, fawn-coloured vinyl binder — zipped shut and filled with the books I had needed to do my homework — I would take up my position and watch for the grille of a Bentley among the grilles of every conceivable other make of car, though none so fine, pouring up over the brow of the hill, out of the Humber Valley.

It's amazing, really, how long past one's most despairing estimate an event unremarkable in every respect aside from being desperately anticipated can occur and yet still fail to be extraordinary. All of a sudden there would be that grille, like something invoked, though not by me, who had tried and failed too many times, and with it would come the re-establishment of the normal course of things, reassuring but no less inadequate than ever, because it wasn't as if I could now be sure I wouldn't be late for school again. And yet it always felt like an undeserved honour, or a lamentable mistake, when the Bentley changed lanes, and slowed, and stopped, just long enough for me to climb, hauling my binder after me, into the back seat, grateful and relieved, and shut the door behind me (a solid impact in a Bentley), and know that at least the next part of my day had begun.

I was not Mr. Powell's only passenger. The other was James Buckerfield, who would already be in the passenger seat when I got in because he lived practically next door to Mr. Powell, in Seneca Heights, on the other side of the Humber River. Buckerfield went to the same school I did but was too senior to care about being late or to let on that he cared or, perhaps owing to his take-no-prisoners performances at the debating regionals, had an understanding with the headmaster. Buckerfield was a large, tall fellow with fleshy lips and a mole like a beauty mark on his left cheek. His fair hair hung over his face in a long bang. His breathing was laboured, his eyes protruded. By the time they pulled over for me, Buckerfield would be deep in political conversation with Mr. Powell, who would be keeping up his end with brief corrective or moderating comments and interjections. As soon as a topic had been dealt with to Buckerfield's satisfaction, he would proceed, with the punctiliousness of an over-controlling seminar leader, to the next.

At the time, I thought of James Buckerfield as Mr. Powell's junior equal. Now I wonder how much Mr. Powell enjoyed discussing politics on his morning commute with a pompous eighteen-year-old. Yet even then I understood, or perhaps only assumed, that he didn't, particularly, for I was conscious of his equanimity, which I admired and hoped one day to emulate in order to address my chronic trembling chin problem when anybody so much as looked at me. While it's possible Mr. Powell was pleased to be giving these two boys a ride to school, I don't think he was. I think he felt he had no choice, though why in my case I have no idea. I can only think it was social pressure of some kind, though it wouldn't have come from my parents who, by virtue of their attractiveness and vivacious all-round good humour when they had a drink in their hand, partied on weekends with the professionals of the town but who when it came down to it were too proud to ask a favour of anybody. Someone else, someone who knew and liked them, must have noticed that, having against all expectations (except my mother's) won a scholarship to a private day school in the city, I would need a daily ride, and this person had had a word with Mr. Powell, who had reluctantly, I assume, agreed. Already taking Buckerfield, who went to the same school, he could hardly refuse.

What impressed me as much as Mr. Powell's equanimity in conversation with Buckerfield and as much as his apparent complete lack of concern for the fix that riding with him put me in was his hair-trigger profligacy with the windshield washer fluid. As soon as the first veil of cement-coloured winter-traffic spray settled on the glass, he would activate the jets and keep them open for what seemed a minute at a time, the powerful wipers slashing away. I imagined a giant tank of washer fluid under the Bentley's hood. Each morning before setting out, Mr. Powell would refill this tank from some even more enormous reservoir, a task that took so long that I was late for school six mornings out of ten.

Clearly, Mr. Powell's willingness to put up with Buckerfield and me was not unrelated to the cleanliness of his windshield or to the compulsion that drove his constant, furious, prolonged rinsing of it. Even at the time, I understood that this was more than a straightforward desire to drive a Bentley with a clean windshield, that for Mr. Powell keeping up his end in a conversation with James Buckerfield for his entire morning commute was only one of many responsibilities that came with being a gentleman, a professional, and a citizen, in whatever order, and these had somehow come to include pulling over to the shoulder of the highway in heavy traffic five mornings a week to pick up a kid he didn't know, the son of people he didn't know, a kid whose chin trembled every time he caught his eye in the rear-view mirror. No wonder Mr. Powell in his tweed suits and crisp blazers, with his smell of Balkan Sobranie pipe tobacco, and his immaculate hair, fingernails, and ears, seemed to me a pressure cooker, ready to blow. As I stared, five mornings a week, at the razor line of his hair at the nape and at his pink, plucked ear and at his aromatic cheek, so smooth and moist and softly reflective of the winter light, with Buckerfield enumerating the pitfalls in store for a new bill before the House, it was all I could do not to reach out and stroke that cheek, while here we were, late again, and my thoughts would go to my hero at that time and for years afterward, until very recently, until that day, in fact, that everything changed for me, the seventeenth-century interpreter and explorer Étienne Brûlé.

‹ ‹ ‹

Partly Brûlé's importance for me had to do with the fact that the emotional centre of my imagination at that time was Seneca Heights, where the Powells and the Buckerfields were neighbours, because it was there that Naomi Kohlmann, the girl I was sick in love with, also lived. Seneca Heights had been built shortly after the Second World War on a height of land overlooking the juncture of the east and west forks of the Humber River. Adjacent to Seneca Heights was a cornfield, at the far edge of which the land fell away to the river. There Naomi Kohlmann and I used to take turns with her mother's gardening trowel, hacking at the ragged edge of the turf, gouging out the yellow gravelly clay under there, in search of Indian artifacts. In the fall we'd scuff through the fallow field for arrowheads and other implements or fragments in stone, slate, bone, tooth. On the desk in the cabin of my boat and subsequently on the kitchen table in my apartment, the stone I use for a paperweight was oval, like an egg, with a quarter-inch-diameter hole the length of it. This is an atlatl, from Seneca Heights, used by the Seneca to give heft to the launch of an arrow or spear. As I have sat at the desk in my boat and later at the kitchen table in my apartment, remembering Mr. Powell and James

Buckerfield, but most of all Naomi Kohlmann, and never forgetting Étienne Brûlé, I have turned this stone over and over in my hand.

Because the cornfield and the embankment along the north edge of it was where Naomi and I found artifacts, we assumed that Seneca Heights had been built next to where the village had been. But one hot summer morning my father got up at the same time I did to declare that there was only one reason a sixteen-year-old would be getting up at 5:30 a.m. in the summer by his own choice, and that was a woman. When I hotly disputed this, informing him that as a matter of fact Byron Colton and I were building a fort down by the river, and liked to get an early start, before the heat of the day, he was not convinced. In the end I was grounded for a week, and it wasn't until 7:30, when he left for work, that I hit my bike running, and by the time I got to Naomi's, her parents and sister had also left for the day, and Byron was already in her bed. When I walked in, he reached across her, saying,

Hold out your hand.

Why should I?

Do it.

I looked at Naomi. Do it, she said. But you're not going to like it.

I opened my hand. Byron dropped the atlatl into it. So? I said, hefting it. What was Naomi talking about? Of course I liked it. Did she think I'd be jealous because it was Byron who'd found it? Of course I was, but I didn't need to let on.

It was under her hedge, where I park my bike, Byron said.

Liar.

It's true, Naomi said. I saw him pick it up.

Okay, Byron said to me. That's enough. Hand it back.

Forget it, Naomi said.

Aww, Byron said. Who found it?

On whose property? Naomi said. Stop whining, Colton. You're such a whiner.

For the rest of that summer and into the fall, I could not get out of my head something that Naomi had understood immediately, but that took me a few days. Seneca Heights had been built not adjacent to that Senecan village but on top of it, or on top of part of it. You'd think that with the attendant pressures of being back in class I'd have moved on, but in my back-seat stew of alienation and resentment, moving on was not an option, and one day in mid-November, when it was stop-and-go on the Gardiner and we were late again, I asked a question of Mr. Powell and James Buckerfield, which I prefaced by characterizing as *the elephant in the car*, though in no way was it the elephant in the car. The elephant in the car was the kid in the back seat. The question? *How did they feel about living on the former site of a Senecan village?* It was the sort of question that you know even before your heart starts to sink as you hear yourself ask it has been morbidly overthought and will fail to achieve its objectives, namely comprehension, respect, chagrin, abject apology — in rapid succession. To drive home my point, in the silence that followed, I sang softly, in a quavering voice,

Oh Canada, our home *on* Native land . . .

Another silence. I could not have said how long. Long enough for me to know that I could easily be ignored here, and then what would I do? Burst into tears? Crow demonically? Throw a screaming fit? To my amazement, as if the Seneca and not the new federal copyright legislation had all along been the subject under consideration in the front seat, as if my interjection, though unorthodox, was worthy grist for the Buckerfield mill, he observed matter-of-factly that the Seneca were a nomadic people, always pulling up stakes. Around here you couldn't dig a posthole, he said, without unearthing Indian relics of some kind. As he made this point, he cast a glance in my direction while failing to meet my eyes, because he was addressing Mr. Powell. You'd be a nomad too, he added, if you hadn't got around to inventing sewers.

To this, with a weird, scathing force, I snarled, They didn't need sewers! And then it was like the time when I was little that the adults at the party said I could have another doughnut if this time I didn't eat the hole. So I carefully left a tiny ring of doughnut around the hole, and when I held it up to show them they erupted in laughter. The only difference this time was that James Buckerfield and Mr. Powell erupted in silence. And then, checking my face in the rearview, Mr. Powell said,

Now, boys. No arguing. I'm sure the savages knew what they were doing.

Each new day that I rode to school with James Buckerfield and Mr. Powell it became clearer to me that, like the developers who had built Seneca Heights, the James Buckerfields and the Mr. Powells of this world moved like midgets amongst the monstrous and spectral hauntings of our Native predecessors, whose traces if they could they would obliterate or ignore — any acknowledgement a market or conversational appropriation. Whereas when the Seneca moved, which they did every decade or so, they took their dead with them, in whatever state of decay, re-ornamented for the trip, for indoor reburial at the new site. Nothing at that time was more evident to me than that this was what I would do: take my dead with me. I would take my dead mother and my dead father and I would certainly take Naomi Kohlmann, were she to die. The only part I wasn't completely sure about was the indoor burial. Possibly some kind of dual-purpose patio arrangement, out back.

‹ ‹ ‹

In the fall and winter of 1992–93, at the age of sixteen, I was riding with Mr. Powell to school, where I was doing poorly in French, Latin, German, and Phys. Ed. In 1608, at the age of sixteen, Étienne Brûlé, physically strong and with an excellent head for languages, left his father's farm on the outskirts of Champigny, not far from Paris, to sail with Samuel de Champlain to the New World. After they had spent two years at Quebec, Champlain sent Brûlé to live among the Huron — enemies of the Seneca — to learn their language and customs. When Champlain next saw Brûlé two years later, he was disgusted to find the boy gone native, in the words of Champlain and of the Récollet and Jesuit Fathers, "filthy," "stupid," "immoral," and "vicious." But as I would argue in my grade twelve essay "Étienne Brûlé: Please Don't Let Him Be Misunderstood," God protects the one who crosses over, particularly if he leaves no written record. For his story, if it is told at all, will be told by those he has left behind, who, confounded by his choice, will find in him their own darkest impulses and discover in his behaviour hostility to everything they had no idea they held as dearly as they did until seeing it so insouciantly, so arrogantly, so scornfully abjured.

Five years later, Champlain set Brûlé another task: to travel in the company of twelve Huron to make contact with the Susquehannock of the upper Susquehanna River in what is now eastern Pennsylvania. The Susquehannock had proposed an alliance with the French and Huron against the Iroquois, of whose Five Nations the Seneca were the nation farthest west. Setting out from Lake Simcoe, Brûlé and his Huron companions travelled up the Holland River, portaged nine miles to the Humber, and made their way down its east branch to where it joins its west below what is now Seneca Heights. Whether at that time there was an inhabited Senecan village overlooking the fork in the river nobody knows, but if there was, Brûlé and his party must have passed unnoticed, perhaps in the night. From there they journeyed the twelve miles of what would come to be called the Carrying-Place Trail to the mouth of the Humber. It was there, or so we were taught at school, that Brûlé was the first white man to see Lake Ontario.

Historians have since changed their minds on this, and though their reasons are obscure and contestable, even I have to admit they might have something. Not one of Brûlé's claims — being the first white man to see Lake Superior, being the first white man to travel the inside passage of Georgian Bay and so being the first white man to see Lake Huron, etc. — has been verified. Also, considering that European artifacts have been found mixed in with Dorset utensils dating back to the 900s, surely other Europeans had laid eyes on Lake Ontario before 1615. In any case, it was at the mouth of the Humber that I would tie up my boat each summer when the promise of summer was over before summer was over, and Étienne Brûlé was the reason why.

‹ ‹ ‹

But I should mention at this point my good friend at that time, the nationally celebrated author Jon Lee Hendricks, because on that particular August day when everything changed for me, it was him I had come to see. And so I made my way from the site of a dubious Étienne Brûlé first, following, more or less, as I have said, the ancient Carrying-Place Trail — which formerly ran along the height of land immediately east of the Humber River and its swampy shore but now lay buried beneath the genteel lawns and homes of Swansea — up Riverside Drive to Humbercrest Avenue, past what is now Étienne Brûlé Park, to Dundas Street and beyond, crabwise into the Junction.

It was a long walk, but I had started early. My destination was the windowless, skylit loft of a five-storey red-brick commercial building on Acme Avenue, access by industrial elevator, and then you climbed an iron ladder inside a corrugated iron cylinder and emerged from the floor, where Jon Lee would be standing by to give me a hand up, but not today. Awkwardly I twisted on the ladder to perch on the edge of the hole and swing my legs up and out, then rolled onto my stomach and got to my feet that way, from my hands and knees, but when I straightened up, with pinpricks of light bursting in front of my eyes, I nearly fell back down the hole. Immediately before me was my teenage sweetheart Naomi Kohlmann, already turning away, not amazed by my sudden appearance from out of the floor but like one who, having heard me climbing up, had approached but finding herself too late to lend a hand was already turning back to what she'd been doing. Naomi Kohlmann, now in her late thirties but younger somehow, looking like nothing so much as a dancer or a gymnast, outfitted for tennis, if tennis were played in black, as perhaps it is in certain Muslim countries such as Kuwait, or Dubai, yet coccyx-tucked and muscle-bound through the shoulders, giving her an attitude of slouching, a pacing truculence. And yet it was not, I suddenly realized, Naomi Kohlmann at all but her sister, *of course*, whom Jon Lee had once, to my astonishment, told me he was seeing. Little Rebecca, now thirty-four or -five, with platinum ringlets, her face not the one I remembered, elusive and never quite in the room, but high-browed and pancaked with makeup — yet surely she had just got up, was she expecting somebody? — the features regular and well spaced across the lower half of the face, the nose long and straight yet a little knocked-to-one-side-looking, the eyes pink-shadowed but haunted, the mouth scarlet.

Rebecca, she said, reaching back her hand while still making to turn away.

I know, I said, in a voice of surprising authority, I know who you are. And I knew that she knew this, for she had recognized me, perhaps had even been told by Jon Lee that I sometimes dropped in unexpectedly, especially in late August when the promise of summer was over before summer was over. As our hands touched, we must have completed a circuit, because right away we started talking, and I knew that, exactly like her sister, but even more so, this was my antagonist twin, the price of whose immediate, scrupulous, unfailing attention to my most casual assertion would be an insistence on palpable evidence of its absolute validity, a refusal to accept any opinion from me that I could not validate to her complete satisfaction, because she would counter it with the full force of her prodigious intelligence rather than admit the slightest possibility that it could be even remotely true. This disposition of mind seemed to arise from no particular anger or animus but from a sheer burning rage to know exactly what was the case and what was not. Rebecca struck me from the moment I came upon her that morning as a true Kohlmann and yet more than this as a woman from the future, or from another planet, a model perhaps for what we all now need to become. She was like one of those bracingly clear- and open-minded but by no means uncritical individuals, often an artist, from some small European country such as Denmark or the Netherlands, or frequently even (strangely enough, or per-haps not strangely at all) Germany, particularly the sort of person who absolutely refuses to accept anything not thor-oughly demonstrated to her high, arguably over-exacting standards.

As it happened, Rebecca had just made herself a pot of coffee. She offered me a cup, along with a slice of toast, which she invited me to spread with almond butter and strawberry jam, which I did. There was also a banana. And so we breakfasted together at Jon Lee's distressed old dining room table, and I can't for the life of me remember how it happened, considering that we had so much to talk about, but we got immediately onto the subject of Étienne Brûlé. Like all true intellectuals Rebecca never shied from an argu-ment, however ugly it promised to become, and no sooner had I uttered the words *tragic fate* with regard to Brûlé than her eyelids lowered, and in a flat voice she said,

By which you mean —

By which I mean, I said quickly, what happened after Champlain sent him to meet the French fleet.

Did he? she said. Keep going.

Which the English had mostly sunk. They then proceeded, with Brûlé as their reluctant guide, to Quebec, where Champlain was forced to surrender the city — or more accurately, small fort, or trading post, or *habitation* as Champlain himself called it — and where Champlain was arrested for transportation to England.

Rebecca looked skeptical at this. Why, I had no idea. It wasn't like I was making it up.

But, I continued, slipping into the special pleading I am sometimes guilty of when it comes to Étienne Brûlé, didn't this mean he was on hand to speak for the lives of the five dozen starving French under Champlain's care? Could Brûlé afford not to co-operate with the English? For all he knew, these were the last days for the French in the New World. The English had already seized what French ships they hadn't sunk. In accompanying the English to Quebec, Brûlé was only being pragmatic, as the Huron were going to need to be if they hoped to trade with the English, who by all appearances in a few years would be the only Europeans around. You take me from my family at the age of sixteen, I assured Rebecca — a little heatedly, for this was a speech I had delivered many times in my mind — and set me down after a sea voyage of many weeks in a strange land with people I can respect, and if I have a heart I will love them, and if I am a decent person I will do what I can for them with the choices available to me, and that is the long and the short of the tragic story of Étienne Brûlé and the Huron.

But even as I advanced this dull and hysterical argument, Rebecca's eyes were lifted upward, to the left, like those of someone who as you hammer away at them is ransacking an upper corner of their mind for a crushing rejoinder. When I paused for breath, immediately going mentally back over what I had just said for points of vulnerability, the way one does, I realized that she was actually looking at something. Twisting around in my seat, I saw what it was: a blinking red light, like an LED light, in the darkness in the gap between the cupboards and the ceiling. Rebecca carried her chair over, and when she stood on it and couldn't reach, I used my own chair to climb up and lift down a video camera, saying, inappropriately, out of shock,

At least it wasn't pointed at the bed.

We set it on the table between us and looked at it.

Rebecca pressed Play.

When it was over, she said, Shit. *Fuck.*

I couldn't agree more, I said, adding, You were fine.

Delete it.

I deleted it, gratefully and with relief. I had never watched myself unawares on video before and was shocked by the phoniness of my vocal and facial mannerisms and physical appearance overall, which were not only ludicrously at odds with how they appear in my mind but unsavoury somehow, as if I am one of those people who try too hard because they have something to hide. What is this unnatural pleading that infects everything I do and say? What am I *begging* for? God, how we give ourselves away, every second of the day.

And we're surprised when yet another seedy charismatic gets away with murder.

Surely Jon Lee wouldn't — I started to say. But he would. That was the thing. This was exactly the sort of thing he would do. This was the kind of friend I had now. Best friend, so-called. And counted myself lucky.

Good Lord, where has all the decency gone?

Even my nemesis throughout adolescence, Byron Colton, commanded a certain hick pride. And didn't Mr. Powell live up to his obligations, at whatever terrible personal cost in windshield washer fluid? And hadn't James Buckerfield saved me from even greater humiliation in the silence after I sang my bit of reworded national anthem, when he spoke as if nothing could have been more relevant to the new federal copyright legislation than Senecan sanitary practices? And ten years later, I happened to be sitting with Buckerfield in a Toronto bar, shortly after he'd returned from Heidelberg with a duelling scar and the affectations of a German officer, and as we chatted I reflected how things between us were now very different from how they were on those mornings we used to ride the Spadina streetcar together, after Mr. Powell had dropped us off outside his office on Adelaide, Buckerfield lecturing me in those days on matters of state, me listening dutifully, not interested, not understanding, sneaking looks at my watch, wondering whom he thought he was talking to, or if he cared, and why he didn't seem the least bit worried that we were going to be late again. And now here we were in this bar, conversing as equals, like old friends, though we weren't, not remotely, but this is how it probably sounded to the barman, although in reality we were just waiting to be joined by some people we both happened to know. I'm sure that if either of us had realized the other was also likely to arrive early, he'd have risked being late. And when casually, in the course of our conversation — I can't remember how exactly it came up — Buckerfield mentioned that he'd always hated my guts, had always found me an insufferable little prig, and even now would have enjoyed nothing more than to smash my face in — at least he was being honest.

How well do you know Jon Lee? I asked Rebecca.

Well enough not to be surprised he'd do something like this.

Where is he?

Visiting a class.

It's a nice day. Did he take his car?

TTC.

Do you drive?

I only asked because at that time, in conscious emulation of Brûlé, I made it a strict rule to travel only on foot or by water — though in exceptional circumstances I did accept lifts in private vehicles, or took cabs — and I feared what Rebecca's excoriating intelligence would make of this information. And even if she remained willing to go anywhere with me at all, she would insist we go somewhere within walking distance, and I'd been walking all morning.

‹ ‹ ‹

We took Jon Lee's car, Rebecca at the wheel. That afternoon she and I spread his ratty old Hudson's Bay blanket over some weeds and picnicked in a farmer's field up past Kleinburg, toward Nashville, on the banks of the Humber, close to where my father is buried. The sun was warm but not hot. There were crickets and grasshoppers and small flies but nothing biting. There were cow patties, but they were dry, and though the hoofprints in the river mud seemed fresh, there were no visible cattle.

Brûlé and his Huron party would have come this way, I told Rebecca. Probably more than that one time. Of course, all this would have been white pine forest. We'd be having our picnic on the deep pine-needle floor of a natural cathedral. Dappled sunlight, lightsome breezes, the whole mystical experience. The kind of experience, I added gratuitously, the Europeans chopped down such forests in order to achieve the wealth and power they needed to build churches to simulate.

We were eating sandwiches and drinking Snapple we had picked up at a convenience store at a highway service centre. A beautiful young Amish woman, or at least a young woman with a rosy complexion wearing a long skirt and an old-fashioned bonnet, was selling fruit at a table by the door. It was something you never see, and you had to ask yourself how on earth somebody had got permission from a faceless multinational for her to do something like that. We bought two apples, which were crisp enough but overpriced and tasteless, and you knew that, deal or no deal, compromises had been made, and not for the first time you wondered how many people have a clue anymore what a real apple is or how it tastes.

When we finished eating, I asked Rebecca if she knew how beautiful she was, though *strange* would have been a more accurate word for me to have used, not that true beauty hasn't always involved a remarkably large component of strangeness. Rebecca's strangeness was not the least bit off-putting, certainly not to me, in fact exactly the opposite, though how much this was a spillover from her sister, whose hold on me had not diminished after twenty-plus years, I hated to think. I'm sure Rebecca's and my radical antagonist attunement had a lot to do with my attraction to her, as it had, of course, with her sister.

Instead of answering my question, which could hardly be called a question, Rebecca went on the offensive, revealing something James Buckerfield had once confided to her. He told her that one morning as I dragged in after me my enormous, book-filled, fawn-coloured vinyl binder across the back seat of Mr. Powell's Bentley, I had left a long scratch in the buttery caramel-coloured leather, which upset Mr. Powell, though he never said anything about it to me.

Why did you have to tell me that? I wailed.

Again Rebecca didn't even pretend to reply. So how do *you* think it was for Brûlé, she asked, after the English deported Champlain?

I should have noticed the way she stressed the *you*. But I was stunned from the blow of her revelation and grateful for an opportunity to return to our discussion concerning Étienne Brûlé.

To understand how it was for Brûlé, I assured Rebecca, you first need to know that at Tadoussac, on board the ship that would transport him to England, Champlain publicly, to their faces, excoriated Brûlé and another interpreter, Nicolas Marsolet, for their apparent complicity in his arrest. And after Champlain was taken away, Brûlé remained among the Huron a ghost of his former self. On days he was sober enough, he must have helped them in their negotiations when they traded with the English, but he'd lost his sponsor and mentor in the New World, and if he'd been a drinker before, he was now constantly drunk. Champlain was gone, and this changed everything —

Which in your view qualifies this sordid tale as a tragedy, Rebecca said.

No, listen, I said. What makes it a tragedy is that Brûlé's helping the English could have turned out to be the right thing for everybody (even Champlain, whose plans in the New World had come to nothing and whom the English would treat justly), and for a while it was, on the face of it, the right thing to do. But what Brûlé had failed to see was that no amount of benefit to the Huron, to the English, to the starving French, nor to his interpreter colleagues, and no earlier harshness of censure of himself by Champlain, would make it possible for him to live with his conscience now that he was an English stooge. It was as if he had said to himself, I can do this, I can hold this pain inside me, for the benefit of us all. But he couldn't. Think Christ in the years immediately preceding the Crucifixion as a falling-down drunk. Because let me be clear, I added, with my old emotion on the subject, this wasn't a man who after he lost his mentor became more debauched than ever, only proving the fatal weakness of his character that had first revealed itself when he went native at eighteen. Étienne Brûlé had tried at every step to do the right thing, with a moral sense he had learned from the Huron. The Huron didn't take it away.

When Rebecca made no response to this, only looked at me appraisingly, once again I mentally went back over what I had just said for points of weakness, and though I found none, when she still didn't say anything, I thought, That was too easy.

So how do you know Jon Lee? I said.

Before answering, she took off her top and lay back and closed her eyes, saying, No, ask me how I knew he'd betray me.

Okay, I said.

She then recounted how last winter Jon Lee had been on a Canada Council poetry jury and took an evening flight to Ottawa for a 9 a.m. meeting. At twenty past, the awards officer called Jon Lee's place in Toronto, and when Rebecca answered he told her that Jon Lee not only had failed to show up for the meeting but hadn't checked into his hotel the night before. Rebecca was about to say that this wasn't like him, something terrible must have happened. And the thing was, it wasn't like him, and yet she found herself unable to say this, and it made no difference that even as she was on the phone with the awards officer Jon Lee walked into the meeting, having come straight off a 7 a.m. bus from Montreal — where his plane had landed at two in the morning, having been diverted on account of fog and freezing rain — because she had just learned something she didn't know until that moment: she didn't trust him. She knew — at some level must have always known — that one day he would betray her. It was only a matter of time.

Rebecca's breasts were extraordinarily beautiful, made strange by thick whorls of blond hair around the nipples.

It's innocence, she said, that thinks it won't be betrayed. Nobody in your Brûlé story was an innocent. And you, you're an adult now, with an adult's experience of life, presumably. So how likely do you think it is really that Brûlé crossed over, whatever that means? Don't you think he could love the Huron and still be a Frenchman, using his Indian relations to advance his wealth and status in New France? Is that so far-fetched? He was obviously intelligent enough to be able to imagine himself both in and out of the straitjacket of any one culture. It's not as if the Huron didn't admire the French, with their *savoir faire*, muskets, sailing ships, and sharp sense of personal style. And what was Brûlé doing with the English in the first place?

I told you that, I said. He ran into them at Tadoussac, when Champlain sent him to meet the French fleet, which they'd mostly sunk.

No, she said. That is not what happened. It wasn't Champlain who sent Brûlé to Tadoussac. He went there with the English.

What? I cried.

It's true, she said. The Jesuit Fathers didn't approve of the example Brûlé's debauched ways were setting for the Huron. They'd had him sent back to France, and from France he made his way to England, not because he knew the French were finished in the New World but because at that point he would have swum the Atlantic to get back to a place where in one year he had access to a hundred times more wealth, freedom, adventure, respect, women, and good times than a French farmer had in a lifetime — a place, moreover, that had become his home, where he could spend his remaining days not ploughing fields and hauling water among the dullards of Champigny but in the company of highly skilled and intelligent men and women. The man was no Christ. Like most of us, but with greater physical and psychological strength, he was a middlingly decent opportunist, which is probably putting it kindly. And like most of us, he got the death he deserved. From England he sailed to the New World with the English and was on board when they attacked the French fleet. After that, he led them to Quebec.

With Champlain gone, she continued, Brûlé lived another four years with the Huron, probably helping them in their negotiations when they traded with the English, and who knows what his conscience was telling him? Imagine, on the other hand, the relief he must have felt to have his life back. It's possible he'd have drunk himself to death even if he hadn't arranged his death another way, but the real remorse, the big remorse, was Huron.

They took on his, I said. His remorse.

No, she said. They had taken on *him*, the burden of him, more than two decades before this, and it was now more than they could bear. In June 1633, when news reached them that Champlain was back in possession of Quebec, they were at a loss. Unlike the English, who had never shown them the slightest respect, Champlain had been their friend and champion, and yet here they'd been going behind his back, both by trading with the English and by allowing the one who'd betrayed him to the English to go on living among them. But what could they do? Wasn't Brûlé one of their own? It wasn't until they learned that he'd been talking to the Iroquois, in an apparent attempt to re-ingratiate himself with the French by organizing Iroquois trade with Quebec, that some Huron, at least, knew what to do. They tortured Brûlé, as they would any enemy, and — to absorb his strength and courage — cooked and ate him, in the traditional way.

But even as they were doing this, something told them that this response, though hallowed, would raise more problems than it would solve. For he was a white man, and what if his death angered Champlain? And it had not stopped being true that, no less than Champlain, Brûlé had been their friend and champion, not to say the lover of their sisters, wives, mothers, and daughters, and so when, at the end of July, Champlain sent a Montaignais friend of Brûlé's to assure them that he had long since stopped considering Brûlé a Frenchman and therefore felt no anger at his death, the Huron were relieved but not entirely, and only for a while.

The next year, Rebecca continued, smallpox wiped out half the population of Touanché, the village where they had tortured and killed Brûlé, and after they set fire to it, as was their custom when it came to smallpox, and were fleeing, looking back they saw that the smoke had assumed the shape of Brûlé's sister, or perhaps his uncle (the two Huron relatives most likely to look out for a wronged family member), whose revenge they understood this was. And everywhere they went, death was with them, and the grieving survivors could never shake the sense that they had committed an unconscionable crime, though whether against one of their own or against a white man who for twenty-three years had been their intimate, they couldn't be sure. But the nagging sense of wrongdoing demoralized them to such an extent that it contributed to their imminent, ultimate defeat and expulsion from their homeland by the Seneca.

But even if it's true that Brûlé wasn't bothered by what he did when he betrayed Champlain, I said, you have to agree it's a sad story.

Listen, she said. Étienne Brûlé chose, for perfectly understandable reasons, to live in circumstances that were never
not perilous. Even so, he didn't die until his desire to go
on living in those circumstances became so great that he
abused the trust of the man and the people who had made it
possible. This is not a story about crossing over, it's a story
about betrayal.

You seem to have done a lot of thinking about Étienne
Brûlé, I said from a mounting sulk.

Whereas you, she said, have never really thought about
him since you've been an adult. For you he's a sentimental
artifact from high school.

With these harsh words, Rebecca removed her shorts
and lay with her head turned to one side and an arm over
her eyes. Her body was fuller than it seemed when clothed,
as bodies often are, the trunk rather short, considering the
length of the legs and the large breasts. Except for her nipples, she was perfectly smooth.

At first I didn't know what to do, so I took off my shirt
and lay down beside her. After a few minutes I said,

You have no right to tell me that.

I do, because it's true. It was all in your mind.

What a terrible thing to say.

The truth is always terrible. She's my sister. I know her.

I loved her.

You loved your idea of her. And now what? You want
to fuck me because you never got to fuck her? And while
you're at it also betray your idea of a best friend?

He doesn't deserve you, I said stupidly, not even knowing
what I was saying, as I drew her farther breast toward my
mouth, and as I touched the tip of my tongue to the nipple,

which stood like a brown traffic pylon in a dust devil of straw or like a novelty hubcap on a wheel of golden thatch, now bristling, I thought, This is not only in my mind, it will be one day, unforgettably, but it isn't now, for it monopolizes my sensorium, and not surprisingly, and yet I couldn't help but wonder how I could have failed to notice the long scratch I had left with my massively heavy fawn-coloured vinyl binder in the buttery caramel-coloured leather seat of Mr. Powell's Bentley, and I wondered too how early in my doglike dependence on his generosity I had inflicted this unwitting damage on his property and why he had never said anything about it to me and what effect, if any, it had on his apparent lack of concern that for weeks at a time, thanks to him, I was late for school at least every second day.

ACKNOWLEDGEMENTS

I am grateful for the warm welcome I have received from Anansi, and more particularly for the skill and professionalism of Janice Zawerbny, John Sweet, Alysia Shewchuk, and Liba Berry. Without them this book would not be what it is.

GREG HOLLINGSHEAD has published six books of fiction, including *The Roaring Girl*, *The Healer*, and *Bedlam*. He has won the Governor General's Award for Fiction and the Rogers Writers' Trust Fiction Prize and been shortlisted for the Scotiabank Giller Prize. Currently professor emeritus at the University of Alberta and director of the Writing Studio at the Banff Centre, in 2011–2012 he served as Chair of the Writers' Union of Canada and in 2012 was awarded the Order of Canada. He lives in Toronto with his wife Rosa Spricer.